AIRSHIP 27 PRODUCTIONS

Dan Fowler: G-Man Volume 2

Edited by Ron Fortier
Associate Editor: Charles Saunders

Cover © 2013 Brian McCulloch
Interior illustrations © 2013 Neil Foster
Production and design by Rob Davis

Published by
Airship 27 Productions
www.airship27hangar.com

ISBN-13: 978-0615820231
ISBN-10: 0615820239

Printed in the United States of America

10 9 8 7 6 5 4 3 2 1

Dan Fowler
G-Man
Volume Two
Contents

Dan Fowler G-Man

in

"The Undercover Puzzle"

by

Derrick Ferguson

New York City
Battery Park
1937

The gasping of the running man was painfully loud to his own ears. He'd been shot before but never like this. It was as if the bullets were actually burning inside of him like coals. The pain was mind-numbing. The last time he'd been shot he'd carried two bullets inside of him for three miles. That had hurt, sure. But nothing like the hellish agony he was struggling against now.

There was no way he was going to make it back to his midtown club. But then again, he shouldn't have been stupid enough to be lured down here. But he had judged the risk worth it. And in any case, he'd secured important evidence that the investigating agent The Bureau sent would be able to find and act on.

The running man stumbled and went head over heels. Tearing the knees and elbows of his three hundred dollar suit. It was already ruined from the blood he'd been losing the last ten blocks he'd run. His legs felt as if they were paralyzed and refused to work. It was as if he had two bags of cold meat hanging from his torso.

And now his hands were trembling and there was no way for him to make them stop. His mouth was dry as Oklahoma dirt but tears flowed from his eyes as if he'd just gotten the news his mother had died.

A heavy foot slammed into the small of his back, pinning him to the ground. "You're a goner, buddy. Nothing can be done for you so you might as well come clean and tell me where it is."

The shuddering, jerking wreck of a man's last snarl of defiance was; "Rot in hell."

The two final gunshots echoed in the eerie silence of Lower Manhattan. The shooter put his weapon away: The Mauser C96. An unusually distinctive weapon to be sure. But he had his reasons for using it. He donned cheap leather gloves, knelt down and searched the dead man's body thoroughly. He found a wallet, stuffed with bills which he helped himself to. But he didn't find what he was looking for judging from the stream of profanity he cut loose with.

No point in hanging around. The dead man didn't have the item he was looking for. However, there were other resources that the killer could tap. He stood up, stripping off the gloves. He discarded them into a sewer grate some five blocks away where they would end up in The East River. He'd have to work fast now. The man he'd killed had been fairly important in New York's underworld and there'd be some heat over his killing. But he enjoyed his work a great deal indeed.

Washington, DC
Department of Justice Building
The Next Day

The gentle knock at the door of his office caught the attention of Dan Fowler. It was his habit to leave his office door open when not engaged in something critical where he required privacy. He was currently finishing up a report involving a case he'd wrapped up just two days ago that had taken him out to Arizona.

The special agent who had knocked gave Fowler an apologetic wave and said, "sorry to bother you, Dan. But The Director said he wanted to see you. He claims it's nothing urgent but you know how he is."

"Indeed I do," Fowler replied, stubbing out his Chesterfield in a chunky square glass ashtray. Even when he said it wasn't urgent whenever The Director summoned an agent to his office it meant that agent should report on the double. "I've got to turn in this report to him anyway. Thanks, Tom."

Fowler closed the folder, walked around his desk and left his office, closing the door, taking a minute to indulge in a bit of pride. The name and title on the pebbled glass door read: INSPECTOR DANIEL FOWLER. It hadn't been so long ago he'd gotten that much sought after promotion. A lot of respect and responsibility went along with it. Such as not being bound by geographical limitations. He went where he was needed. In a lot of ways he was considered by many of his fellow agents in the Federal Bureau of Investigation to be The Director's chief troubleshooter.

Fowler walked down the wide hallway. Six foot two of muscle. Dark haired, skin tanned a healthy bronze he nodded back to those who greeted him in passing. He arrived at The Director's office. The reception office was staffed by a single male secretary who looked up from his typewriter and waved Fowler in. "He's expecting you, Inspector Fowler."

The pebbled glass of The Director's officer was wider and heavier than the door of Fowler's officer and simply read; DIRECTOR, DIVISION OF INVESTIGATION. No name. None was needed. To all who worked for The FBI he was "Mr. Director." Or even more simply; "Director"

The Director favored white double breasted suits. He appeared to be no older than in his forties, with steady brown eyes and a stern, serious face. He stood in front of the huge casement windows looking out onto Pennsylvania Avenue. Some might have worried that in that blindingly white suit and standing so boldly in front of those windows that The Director was deliberately making himself a target. No fear of that. Fowler knew that the glass of the windows was of a special type developed by a good friend of the Bureau. From the outside looking in, whatever a potential sniper saw was five feet to the left of where it actually was. And since the glass was bullet resistant as well the chances of The Director being hit were slim and none. "Good of you to come so quickly, Fowler. Is that the file on the Lorca case?"

"It is, Mr. Director." Fowler placed it on the polished mahogany desk and stepped back, hands folded behind him. He wouldn't dream of sitting down unless and until given permission.

"Go ahead and make yourself comfortable, Fowler. Smoke if you want. I've got something of a situation here and frankly, I badly need your help."

Fowler seated himself and took out a jeweled cigarette case from the inside pocket of his jacket. "Are you all right, sir?"

"I don't know, Fowler. I honestly don't know." The Director turned back to look out the window onto Pennsylvania Avenue. "How much do you know about Harry Butterfield?"

Fowler thought for a minute before speaking. He had excellent memory recall. The Director liked to boast that Fowler had a brain like a file cabinet. "He operates out of New York now. Butterfield learned his trade working with Fat Charley Makley. Robbing banks, bootlegging. Butterfield didn't like the Midwest, though and came east. Probably kept him alive this long. If he'd stayed out there in Missouri or Indiana he probably would have been killed by one of our lads long ago. He owns a nightclub in Manhattan. Keeps his hand in with the bootlegging, illegal gambling. He may even be dealing a little dope on the side."

"You ever met him?"

Fowler again thought before speaking, blowing out cigarette smoke. "I know he was involved with that smuggling ring working down in Miami back in '35. Remember them?"

"I remember that you put them out of business." The Director turned around and his expression was plainly troubled. "But you've never laid eyes on Butterfield in person?"

"No. Seen pictures of him but that's about it." Fowler didn't let the impatience he was feeling show on his face. He'd never seen The Director act like this before. Usually he got down to business right away. Whatever this assignment was, it was different from any other he'd given Fowler.

The Director turned away from the windows and walked over to his desk, seated himself behind the gleaming mahogany expanse and folded his big, powerful looking hands on his stomach. "What I'm about to tell you is known to only three people: The President of The United States, The Attorney General and myself."

"I'm listening, sir."

"Harry Butterfield was an undercover agent for us."

"How'd you get a bad egg like Butterfield to turn?"

The Director smiled thinly. "That's just it: Harry Butterfield always was an agent. There was no need to turn him because he was on our side from Day One. In fact, Butterfield wasn't his real name. It was Brent Coleman."

"Mr. Director, you mean to tell me that Butterfield…excuse me, Coleman was undercover for over five years? I find that hard to believe. I've either met or know of all the undercover men we have in play and I'm positive I've never heard of this Coleman."

"That's because I took him out of the Academy before he graduated. The idea was to put an undercover agent in the field before he was in the system. This way there was no record of him having been an agent. No chance of him being recognized as a Fed because he would never *have* been one." The Director allowed himself to take some pleasure in the surprised look on Fowler's face. Fowler had the tendency sometimes to come off as a know-it-all. And while The Director appreciated the extent of Fowler's encyclopedical knowledge he couldn't deny that it was fun to be able to surprise Fowler once in a while with something he *didn't* know.

The Director continued; "I know Brent's dad well. We were partners back in the late 20's. One night when I was having dinner at their house, I outlined the plan I had. I honestly wasn't thinking of Brent for it but he jumped at the opportunity. His dad also was eager for Brent to take the job. I was reluctant but I made sure that Brent knew the risks. No one would know he was an undercover agent. He was totally on his own. I took him out of the Academy a few days later, citing him as psychologically unfit and supervised the rest of his training myself. A little cosmetic surgery, a year in Dannemora and Harry Butterfield was ready for his life of crime."

"I'm beginning to understand a few things," Fowler said. "From time to time you'd come up with these insights into the workings of this gang or that. Or how certain organizations operated. Or the personal habits of major criminals. It always mystified me as how you got that information."

"Brent and I would meet every three months. Always a different city, never the same one twice. Sometimes I'd spend two or three days debriefing him. That's how much information he had. And I had to transcribe the information myself because I couldn't take anybody else with me."

Fowler nodded. "And you would usually tell us agents you were on a hunting trip when you had to meet with Coleman."

"It wasn't exactly a lie, Fowler." The Director said with a wink. Then he became serious again. "But the entire situation has changed now."

"Coleman's dead," Fowler said flatly.

"How'd you guess?"

"No guess. The only reason you would have for breaking such secrecy is if there was no reason to maintain Coleman's cover. My guess is he's been murdered."

"He caught four in Manhattan. I want you there to investigate and find out what happened and why he was killed." The Director leaned forward. "I want Bob Coleman's boy to be buried with the full honors he deserves, Fowler. Brent Coleman gave up five years of his life in service to his country and he should have nothing less."

"But you want to be sure that he actually *was* still working for you and maybe hadn't been undercover *too* long?"

"I've got legitimate concerns. He called off our last debriefing session which was supposed to have been in Kansas City last month. Said he was on the trail of something big and couldn't let it get cold. I didn't think anything of it at the time. Brent had called off or postponed meetings before. No big deal. But now-"

"-now you're wondering."

"Fowler, you've known men who were undercover for a lot shorter period of time than Brent was and you've seen what it did to them. If Brent Coleman *was* dirty then he'll be buried as Harry Butterfield. But I need to be sure. I wouldn't trust this with anybody else except you."

"Of course I'll take the assignment, sir." Fowler stood up and reached across the desk to shake hands.

"I suppose you'll need Kendal to assist."

Fowler grinned. "Larry's a good man to have at my back, sir. You know how well we work together."

The Director sighed. "I can't deny the record of success the two of you have had. I just can't help but wonder how an FBI Inspector finds all the free time he seems to have to spend playing polo, tennis, golf and nightclubbing. I suppose you'll want Miss Vane as well?"

"I've got a special job in mind for her on this job, sir."

"Take her, take 'em both," The Director waved his hand in dismissal. "Just come back with what I want to hear, Fowler."

"With all due respect, Mr. Director…I'll come back with the truth. Whether it's something you want to hear or not."

"I don't see why we just couldn't have flown from Washington to New York." Larry Kendal groused. "Not that I mind the driving but the way you make this assignment sound, time isn't exactly on our side." Kendal was in the driver's seat, his window open and his elbow sticking out. Fowler rode shotgun and had kept himself busy during the four hour drive by reading Brent Coleman's extensive file which had come from The Director's personal safe in his house.

It made for some fascinating reading and Fowler's respect for the murdered undercover agent went up several notches. Whatever else he may have done, Coleman/Butterfield had done more than his share to put a lot of bad customers behind bars where they belonged.

Without looking up from the file Fowler said, "I know you like to drive and I'd rather we use a car we know and we're familiar with rather than borrow one from the New York office. We know this car and its capabilities as well as we know our own shoes."

Kendal grinned at his partner. "You don't want to have to go looking for the clutch if we've got to get away in a hurry, I take it?"

"You take it right, feller."

Kendal concentrated on navigating the big automobile through the Manhattan traffic. Larry Kendal looked more like a professional playboy or tennis pro than an FBI Inspector with his dark hair, suave good looks and olive skin. Indeed, Kendal's favorite pastimes were playing tennis, golf or polo at Arlington's prestigious Haversham Country Club. These activities gave Kendal a higher profile than The Director would have preferred as the newspaper gossip columns loved to run pictures of "The Playboy Agent" as they liked to call Kendal. But The Director let it go because there was no denying that Kendal was an extremely capable agent. Even more so when partnered with Fowler.

"Who's the Assistant Director in Charge here?" Kendal asked.

"His name's George Corley. I know him. Good man. Capable but just a little too inquisitive. The Director was adamant that he not know the real reason for our investigation."

"So what are you going to tell him?" Kendal navigated a left turn.

"We suspect that Butterfield was killed by a torpedo from California who may have killed an informant of ours. We're here to see if we can tie in the two killings."

"Smooth." Kendal chuckled. "And here we are."

Shortly Fowler and Kendal were sitting in the office of Assistant Director Corley. George Corley was short but had a good athletic build on him. His coffee colored eyes were clear, honest and full of curiosity. He obviously took great care of his thick, luxurious black hair.

"Fowler. Good to see you again." Corley said as he shook hands with him.

"Thank you, Assistant Director. This is my partner, Inspector Larry Kendal."

"The Playboy Agent, eh? Heard a lot about you, Kendal."

"I bribe 'em to say it all, sir," Kendal replied with a grin as he shook hands.

"Sit down, sit down and tell me more about this investigation of yours. The Director wasn't very informative over the phone. Said you'd give me the lowdown once you got here."

"There really all that much to inform you of, sir. The Butterfield killing may have been done by a California torpedo who blasted one of my confidential informants. I'd just like to see the autopsy report, talk to a few of Butterfield's people. Maybe I can find a connection to tie the two killings together."

"I see. And why would you think this California trigger man blasted your snitch?" Corley was looking shrewdly at Fowler. The look wasn't lost on Fowler. There was something here and Corley wanted to know what it was.

"Fowler pointed at bullet holes…"

"Information from another confidential informant, sir."

"I see." But Corley really didn't. "Very well, then. Let's get down to the morgue and Dr. Wexel can give you his report."

It wasn't far to the morgue. Corley led the two agents down two wide flights of marble stairs to the basement where he pushed open the double doors and introduced them to Dr. Wexel, a gray eyed man slightly smaller than a medium sized mountain. Dr. Wexel smiled as he took in the looks given him by Fowler and Kendal. "What's the matter, boys? Never seen a doctor before?"

"Not one that looks big enough to wrestle a gorilla," Kendal admitted.

"Matter of fact, wrestling was how I put myself through medical school. I remember-"

Fowler coughed theatrically and Dr. Wexler quickly brought himself back to the subject at hand. "Sorry, Inspector Fowler. If you'll step over here I'll give you my report."

The body was lying on a metal dissection table. A sheet covered it. Fowler flipped back the sheet with a practiced twist. He took off his tan fedora, tossed it on a nearby table and proceeded to examine the body himself with his eyes and hands.

"Cause of death was from four 7.63mm bullets, fired at close range. Two in the stomach, two in the back."

Fowler looked up sharply at Kendal. "That's Mauser ammunition."

Kendal nodded in confirmation. "The C96, I think. The Broomhandle. Haven't seen one of those in years."

Fowler pointed at the bullet holes in the body's abdomen. "What do you make of this strange discoloration, Dr. Wexler?"

The huge doctor scratched the back of head while his face registered honest puzzlement. "I truly can't say, Inspector Fowler. I chalked it up to the unusual ammunition used. Most of the bullet wounds I see here are from .45 or .38 slugs. This is the first time I've seen bullet wounds made by this type of ammunition."

"Where are those bullets?" Fowler asked.

"Right here." Wexler indicated that they should follow him over to a workbench. The four bullets were secured inside a small jar. Fowler took the jar and using a pair of small forceps provided by Wexler removed one of the bullets. Fowler went over to a microscope and placed the bullet on the stage and looked at it for several long minutes.

Corley was impatient, Wexler intrigued and Kendal merely stood with a huge smile on his face. He was familiar with Fowler's mood when he was hot on the trail of something and whatever it was that was so interesting about that bullet would no doubt be a revelation.

Fowler stood up straight. "I'll be damned," he said quietly. "Dr. Wexler, you should get a look at this. If you ever run into a similar case you'll know what you're dealing with."

Wexler took Fowler's place at the microscope and peered at the bullet. "What am I looking at, Inspector?"

"Notice the unusual purplish color of the bullet?"

"Now that you mention it, yes. Again, I thought it was due to the unusual ammunition used."

"In a way it is. Good thing you handled those bullets with rubber gloves or you'd be as dead as Butterfield. Those bullets were soaked in a solution for three full days before they were used." Fowler regained his fedora, replaced it on his head. "A solution made from the *Tugug* Orchid. An Orchid grown and used by The Hip Ling Tong."

Corley looked at Fowler in disbelief. "Poisoned bullets? You must be joking!"

Fowler nodded at the cold body lying on the even colder metal table. "Ask Butterfield there if he thinks it's a joke. I've run into the Hip Ling Tong before-"

"-that's an understatement if I ever heard one," Kendal muttered.

Fowler continued as if he hadn't heard his partner. "Those poisoned bullets are one of their special tricks to make sure that anybody who crosses them doesn't survive. No matter where the bullet hits you, you're a dead man. You may take what would normally be a flesh wound but with one of these bullets it doesn't matter. Whoever killed Butterfield works for the Hip Lings. And they wanted to make sure he was dead. They were taking no chances on him getting away and talking."

Corley's face was flush with excited impatience. "I *knew* there was more to this than you were letting on! Okay, Fowler, let's have it all! Who was Butterfield, really? Who was he working for? How'd he get mixed in with a Tong? And what's your real assignment here in New York?"

"Thank you for your co-operation, Dr. Wexler." Fowler ignored Corley as if he weren't even there and turned to shake hands with the big doctor. "I strongly advise you put those bullets in a sealed box and ship it to Headquarters in Washington. For your own safety continue to handle them with gloves on. We'll take it from there."

"As fast as I can, Inspector!"

Corley stepped between them. "You wouldn't be ignoring a superior, would you, Fowler? An Assistant Director, no less?"

"No, sir. I was just thanking Dr. Wexler for his help."

"Then I want you and Kendal in my office right now and I want to know exactly what your assignment is and what your orders are!"

Fowler's voice was as blunt and as subtle as a thrown monkey wrench. "With all due respect, sir...I work for The Director. Not you. If there's anything about my assignment you want to know, you talk to him. Kendal, c'mon. We've got work to do."

Once they were back in their car and Kendal was steering into the congested Manhattan traffic did he chuckle and say; "kinda hard on the guy back there, weren't you, Dan?"

"I can't abide anyone who looks to make a reputation by exceeding orders without a good cause. Corley's a good man but he's always been just a bit too nosy for my comfort. He's always angling to work a case that he thinks will get him in good with The Director and bump up his profile. And I was following The Director's orders to not inform Corley of the true purpose of our assignment."

"Hey, I'm right behind you 100%. You know that. But you could have been a little more diplomatic about it, y'know."

"I have a job to do. I don't have time to be diplomatic."

"So what's our next move? I hope you say lunch 'cause I could do with a juicy steak right about now."

"Let's check out Butterfield's place first. The file said he had digs in the Ridgeley Arms over on Central Park West. We'll give his place the once over and see if we can pick up any leads. Then we'll grab some chow and check out his club."

"Sounds like a plan to me."

Harry Butterfield's primary residence was a tenth floor suite located in The Ridgeley Arms was no more than a brisk fifteen minute walk from Central Park West on 79th Street. Kendal parked the big sedan right in front of the polished glass doors, almost knocking over the big red NO PARKING sign.

A burly doorman, face darkening with anger under the stingy brim of his cap bustled up to the sedan. "Can't you read, dope? The sign says NO PARKING and we mean it!"

Kendal flashed his badge. "Simmer down, Admiral. How can you move so fast in that getup?" Indeed, the doorman's uniform was so busy with gold braid, large faux gold buttons and scrambled eggs that just the jacket alone looked as if it weighed fifty or sixty pounds. The doorman looked unhappy upon seeing the badge.

"Hey, look…we don't need any trouble here, okay?"

"What kind of trouble do you think we're bringing?"

The doorman looked even unhappier. "Well, first those cops went on up to Mr. Butterfield's suite and-"

Fowler and Kendal swapped glances. "How long ago did these police officers go upstairs?" Fowler demanded.

"Maybe fifteen minutes ago."

"You saw their ID?"

"Well…no…they *said* they were cops…"

Kendal groaned and seized the doorman by the arm and half-dragged him into the splendidly gleaming marble and glass lobby. Fowler was already inside and heading for the stairs. Kendal pointed at the telephone behind the doorman's desk. "Call the local precinct. Ask them if they've sent detectives here or know anything about detectives being sent here to Butterfield's suite for any reason. If not, tell them you have two Federal officers here requesting backup. Fowler and Kendal. Got that?"

"Yessir!"

Kendal took the elevator up to the tenth floor and his .38 Colt automatic was in his hand when the elevator door slid open. Fowler was already in the hall and even though he'd just run up ten flights of stairs he didn't seem to least bit winded. Fowler's weapon of choice was a .357 blue steel revolver. Fowler and Kendal spoke not a word, communicating with their eyes and hand signals. The two agents had worked together for so long that it was almost as if they read each other's mind. They made their way down the wide white and jade green corridor toward the double Adamesque style doors at the end. The doors were slightly ajar and Fowler nudged the doors open wider with a foot. They could hear noises inside the suite. Noises both men were familiar with. Somebody was searching the place and not being very subtle about it. Fowler wished the foyer weren't so brightly lit but that couldn't be helped. He crept into the foyer. Kendal slipped past him, took up a covering position while Fowler moved past him, deeper into the suite.

The living room looked big enough to play soccer in. Huge white couches formed a U around a central, circular fireplace. A slim man in a dark suit was busy tearing up the couches with a knife that looked more suited to skinning bears than slicing up furniture.

Fowler cocked his revolver and ordered; "Drop the knife and put your hands over your head! This is the FBI!"

The knife man's head whipped upwards, took in the sight of the massive barrel of the .357 pointed at him and amazingly, leap-frogged right over the couch he'd been mutilating and ran deeper into the suite.

Fowler took off after him, Kendal close behind. A shot rang out and a slug whizzed by Fowler's cheek. He whirled and fired twice at the shooter, who stood just inside a guest bedroom doorway. The heavy .357 shells shattered the door jamb, sending a blizzard of wood shavings into the face of the shooter, who screamed and stumbled backwards, firing wildly.

Kendal finished him off with two well placed shots right in the chest. The shooter screamed wordlessly and toppled over backwards.

The knife man was doing his fair share of yelling as well. There was another man in the suite and this one emerged from the master bedroom. Fowler got a good look at him. Dark, muscular. It was hard to place where he might have come from. He wore good clothing. Not expensive but not cheap either. His hair was slicked down tight against his skull. He seemed vaguely Asian but at the same time, Fowler thought he might have been Egyptian.

The really important thing was the weapon he was pointing at Fowler and Kendal: A broomhandle Mauser.

"Larry, move!" Fowler ordered and dived behind a couch, followed by Kendal. Bullets from the Mauser whammed into the couch which thankfully was thick enough to give them adequate protection.

"How much you want to bet that those bullets are poisoned just like the ones that came out of Butterfield?" Fowler asked.

"I'll take your word for it," Kendal replied grimly. "Shall we give the boy something to think about?"

"You go left, I'll go right," Fowler agreed. "One, two, THREE!"

On THREE, Fowler sprang to his feet with that dazzling athletic ability he had demonstrated on so many other dangerous occasions and while running toward the kitchen, snapped off three shots that drove the Mauser wielding killer back into the master bedroom. Kendal was coming up and around from the left side. The idea was that Fowler would keep the killer pinned down while Kendal got in close enough to either take the shot or force the killer to drop his weapon.

That plan quickly went sour as the knife man emerged with a Browning automatic rifle in his hands and enthusiastically began spraying the living room. Kendal was forced to dive back behind a couch as the bullets tore through furniture, knocked fist sized holes in the walls and doors leading to the kitchen, where Fowler was lying on the floor, covering his head as mangled plaster, ruined china and chips of wood flew like angry bees in the air.

"C'mon, Rome!" The knife man yelled. The Mauser wielding killer, who apparently was named Rome, nimbly ran from the master bedroom and aided by the covering fire from the knife man ran through the living room. Kendal valiantly snapped off two futile shots before he was forced back to the relative safety behind the couch, which was now smoldering as the heat from the bullets caused the cotton stuffing of the cushions to ignite.

Fowler scrambled to his feet and kicked down what was left of the kitchen door. The knife man was frantically trying to slam home a fresh clip into the BAR. "Drop it!" Fowler ordered.

The knife man had finally gotten the clip in and swung the barrel of the rifle up just in time to catch two bullets from Fowler's gun right in the chest. He stumbled backwards from the sledgehammer impact and thumped against a cream colored wall. He slowly slid downwards, leaving a broad blood smear. The BAR thumped to the now gore streaked carpet.

Kendal was gone, chasing Rome, no doubt. Fowler found a large crystal pitcher and filled it with water. He poured it over the smoldering couch to douse the fire.

Kendal returned to the suite, disgust on his face.

"Got away?"

"I've never seen anybody run as fast as that guy. By the time I hit the door on this floor he was on the fifth floor. He pegged a few shots at me and since I didn't feel like being poisoned today I figured I'd let him have his way for now."

Fowler nodded. "We've got these two." He indicated the two dead men. "Maybe we can get a lead on our boy after we identify these two."

"HANDS UP!" a voice boomed. Uniformed New York policemen were suddenly flooding the suite, guns drawn.

Fowler grinned. "Nothing like backup, is there, Larry?"

It took some time to get things sorted out in the bullet-ridden suite. Even after Fowler and Kendal showed their identifications the tall, imposing sergeant insisted that Assistant Director Corley be summoned to make a personal ID of the two FBI agents. Fowler was fairly well known to the NYPD but this sergeant apparently wasn't taking any chances. Newshounds were choking the lobby, demanding to know why no major arrests had been made in the wake of a major gun battle in one of the swankiest residential buildings in New York. Before he turned his two suspects loose he wanted to make damn sure of whom they were.

Corley arrived with a smirk and superior attitude. He entered the suite and looked around the living room, whistled low and long. "Who were you and Kendal shooting it out with up here, Fowler? An army regiment?"

"You know this gentleman, Mr. Corley?"

"Sure, Harris. Inspector Fowler is practically The Director's right hand man. Where's the other one?"

"In the kitchen with some of my men watching him." Harris gave a quick description of Kendal to which Corley nodded in confirmation.

"That's Kendal. They're okay."

"I'll still have to investigate this, sir. There are two dead men here that have to be identified."

"You have any idea who they are?" Fowler wanted to know. Harris shook his head in a negative.

"I know most of our homegrown talent but neither one of their faces rings any bells for me. Maybe they're out of towners, brought in just for this job." Harris looked meaningfully at Fowler. "Whatever that job was."

Corley placed a hand on Harris' shoulder. "Give us a few minutes alone, okay?"

Harris grudging withdrew while Corley stepped closer to talk quietly with Fowler.

"Okay, Fowler. Time to stop being hardnosed about this and come clean.

"He stumbled backwards from the…impact…"

What's this really all about? Who was Butterfield? One of us? What are you investigating? What are your orders?"

Fowler lit a cigarette he took from his jeweled cigarette case. "Exactly what I told you earlier, Assistant Director. No more. No less."

"Dammit, Fowler, I just got you off the hook with the NYPD!"

"With all due respect, sir, no you didn't." Fowler blew out smoke. "Sergeant Harris couldn't have held Kendal and I and you know it. Him asking you down here to make a personal identification was simply his way of covering himself with the press and his superiors."

"It's not right that I be left out of your investigation, Fowler! The Director should have informed me of your assignment here and put me in charge!"

"And I again respectfully suggest that you call The Director and air your grievance with him, sir. Not me. Now if you'll excuse me…" Fowler turned and walked away from a seething Corley and went into the kitchen which was filled with the sounds and smells of cooking.

Larry Kendal was at the stove, pan frying T-bone steaks and scrambling eggs. His suit jacket and hat were lying on a chair. His sleeves were rolled up, tie was loosened and he was looking as if he was having the time of his life. Three cops were at the kitchen table, shoving eggs and steak into their mouths as if they hadn't eaten all day long. Kendal grinned at Fowler. "Just in time, partner. Pull up a chair. You like your steak medium, right?"

Fowler couldn't help but grin back. "That appetite of yours just won't stop, will it?"

"Hey, Butterfield's got a whole freezer full of meat he doesn't need and we need to keep our strength up. And I didn't see any harm in sharing with New York's Finest." Kendal shrugged. "Sit. Eat."

Fowler had to admit; it *did* smell awfully good. "I guess there's nothing wrong with having a quick bite before we search the place ourselves…"

The police finally left the two agents alone and they went to work. FBI agents were trained extensively in the art of concealing information and now that Fowler and Kendal knew that Butterfield had actually been an agent, they knew where to look. It was Fowler who found something after thirty minutes of searching. "Here, Larry."

Kendal walked into the bedroom. Fowler was standing by the bed, holding up a key. A small folding knife in his hand. Butterfield had sewn the key into the mattress.

"Looks to me to be a safety deposit box key, Dan."

"That's exactly what it is."

"How many safety deposit boxes are there in New York City, you reckon?"

"I wouldn't even venture to guess," Fowler replied, looking at the shining key lying in the palm of his hand. "It looks brand new. Hardly ever used."

"Which means that whatever is in it, Butterfield put it in there recently."

"Good point. Let's finish up here and head to midtown. I suppose that since your gut is full I can expect some honest work out of you now?" Fowler grinned at his partner.

"We're going to Butterfield's club now, I take it?" Kendal asked.

"You take it right, feller."

"Good. Nothing I like better after steak and eggs than a dry martini."

The garish lime green neon sign of BUTTERFIELD'S was already lit, splashing its glow over West 47th Street as Kendal parked the sedan across the street. Fowler and Kendal climbed out, sizing up the place before crossing the street and going on in. The green color motif extended to the inside as there seemed to be four or five shades of green competing for which was the biggest eyesore.

"Who designed this joint?" Kendal muttered. "A deranged leprechaun?"

The maitre d intercepted them in the foyer. Calling him a maitre d was about as appropriate as calling Dillinger a freelance financial redistribution agent. "We don't want no feds lookin' fer trubble in here," he growled. He was very thick, obviously well muscled and his bullet head looked as if it could take more than few knocks.

"What you actually mean to say is: 'we don't want any federal officers looking for trouble'" Fowler replied. "If you're going to work with the public you really have to articulate clearly."

"Listen, bub-"

Fowler reached out almost lazily and seized the maitre d's right wrist and bent it in a direction wrists were not designed to bend in. The maitre d's face immediately darkened with pain. But his eyes glowered at a benignly smiling Fowler who said softly: "You're going to escort my friend and me to the bar. You're going to tell the bartender that our drinks are on the house. Then you're going to go get whoever took over this dump after Butterfield got his and tell him that Dan Fowler wants to see him." Fowler let go of the man's wrist.

The look in the maitre d's eyes plainly revealed that he'd heard of Fowler. Rubbing his outraged wrist he jerked his head toward the marble and glass horseshoe shaped bar. "Right dis way, gent'men." Fowler and Kendal followed him, taking off their fedoras as they did so.

The maitre d motioned for the bartender. "Rudy, set these gent'men up with whatever they want. And their money's no good here, see?"

"Gotcha, Rolly."

Fowler still had that benign smile on his face as he said; "I think you're improving in your job all the time, Rolly."

Rolly gave Fowler one last glare before turning away and headed for the rear of the club. Kendal chuckled as he handed Fowler a Scotch and water. He sipped from his own martini glass. "You have such a persuasive way about you."

Fowler raised his glass in salute to his partner. "It's the company I keep." He took a sip and let his sharp eyes roam over the club. The dance floor had maybe a dozen couples keeping it active and the waiters were kept hopping serving food and drinks. The place wasn't as lavish and other Manhattan clubs but neither was it a dump as Fowler had said.

"I'm surprised you didn't come here first," Kendal remarked, signaling that the bartender should hit him again.

"I didn't have to. Take a look down at the far end of the bar."

Kendal did so and he chuckled in amusement. "I shoulda known. When did she get here?"

"Earlier this afternoon. I told her to fly up from Washington, find a perch here in the club and keep her ears and eyes open." Fowler smiled and took another sip. "Never hurts to have an ace up your sleeve."

Fowler's 'ace' was a five foot five package with a figure that movie actresses would have killed their own mothers for. She wasn't beautiful but she was that type of cute that made her even more attractive than women more glamorously gorgeous. Her face was framed by a glistening halo of frosty golden hair and her lips were invitingly plump. Sally Vane had worked with Fowler for quite some time now and he relied on her skills and talents just as much as he relied on Kendal's. And with good reason. Sally had a brain that was more dangerous than any of the weapons she carried and she had more sheer guts than most men Fowler knew.

"You think she's found out anything?"

"You know better than to ask that, Larry. Sally can get more information out of a man by crossing her legs than a Chicago cop with a blackjack."

Rolly returned, his expression not having changed a bit. "Mr. Dunn says come on back to the office."

"You first, Rolly," Fowler ordered. "Seeing as how we don't know the way."

Rolly grudgingly led the two agents past the dance floor and the small round tables circling it to the rear of the club. Kendal watched their backs and signaled Fowler that nobody was closing in on them from behind. Apparently this Mr. Dunn had decided to play it square. Rolly passed by several closed doors and stopped at one that was significantly more decorated than the rest with a delicate clamshell motif etched into the surface. Rolly knocked. "Come!"

Rolly opened the door and held it open for Fowler and Kendal who brushed past him and went on in. Nobody else was in the room except for a short, broad-shouldered man with large green eyes and very black hair. He was standing at a private bar, pouring himself a drink. Kendal turned and indicated to Rolly that he should leave and shut the door. Then Kendal positioned himself so that he'd have a clean line of fire should any one burst in unexpectedly. He also could cover Fowler if a gunman emerged from a hidden panel in the wall.

"You Dunn?" Fowler asked.

"That's me. Louis Dunn. And you'd be Dan Fowler, the FBI's golden boy. Why aren't you out protecting this great country of ours from the bad guys?"

"What was your relation to Harry Butterfield?"

"What's your interest?"

Fowler's eyes turned hard just that fast. "I think maybe you've forgotten how this is supposed to go, Dunn. I ask the questions and you answer them. Not the other way round."

Dunn raised his hands in mock surrender. "Hey, hey…you don't have to be that way. I've heard stories about you, Fowler. I know you're tough. But I'm co-operating, aren't I? You don't see any of my boys here, do you? But you can't expect me not to be curious when the FBI comes around asking about my dead partner." .

"That's all you and Butterfield were? Partners?"

Dunn took a sip of his bourbon before answering. "I wanted to stay in the background and Harry didn't mind being the public face. I don't like the spotlight myself. Guess I'll have to find myself a new partner."

"Butterfield have a lot of enemies?"

"You know just as well as I do that you can't be in the rackets without bending a few noses out of joint. But things have been real quiet lately. Business is good. Nobody wants to start something that could bring the heat down on us all. Mind you, I'm not saying that Harry didn't have his share of guys who didn't throw their hats in the air and cheer when they heard he'd purchased agricultural real estate. What I'm saying is that nobody disliked him enough to do it now."

"Maybe somebody killed him over a woman?"

Dunn cocked his head to the side, looking at Fowler shrewdly. "What are you really here about, Fowler?"

"I'm investigating Harry Butterfield's death because he was killed the same way one of my informants was. Same weapon, same method. What I'm trying to find out is why the same torpedo would kill your partner and my informant."

Dunn shrugged carelessly. "Can't help you there, Fowler. But for what it's worth, I do hope you catch up to whoever gave it to Harry. He was okay."

Fowler gave Dunn a long searching look before turning to leave. Kendal held the door open for him as Fowler walked out. Kendal closed the door and the two agents fell into step. "Almost makes you wish you didn't have to lie to the guy, huh?" Kendal asked.

"He really did like Butterfield, Larry. If he had anything at all that he thought would help us catch who killed him, he'd have told us. But we have to keep up the pretense that Butterfield was a gangster while we're investigating this case."

"I hope like hell he was straight, Dan."

"Me too. Let's get together with Sally and see what she's got."

"Butterfield had a girl he was real sweet on. Word is he was going to marry her soon." Sally Vane knocked back another Southern Screw as she made her report to Fowler who occupied the stool next to her. "Some of the other girls who worked here weren't too happy about that. Butterfield was quite the playboy before Sandra came along."

"Sandra?"

"Sandra Wheeler. Cute trick from Montana. Came to the big bad city eighteen months ago, walked in off the street hungry and humble. Butterfield gave her a job as hat check girl. Not too long after that they were stepping out. Didn't make Sandra popular with her co-workers."

"She a person of interest to us?"

Sally nodded. "I would say so. She hasn't been seen since Butterfield got his."

Fowler smiled. "But you know where to find her, I bet."

Sally reached into her silver clutch bag and withdrew a piece of paper. "She's got an apartment here in Manhattan and her folks live in Brooklyn."

Fowler impulsively leaned forward and kissed her on the cheek. "What would I do without you, Sally?"

"Probably get yourself killed."

It didn't take Kendal long to drive from the nightclub to Sandra Wheeler's apartment building on East 28th Street. The three agents made their way upstairs to her third floor apartment. Fowler let Sally go on ahead. He was hoping that Sandra would open up to another woman, especially one who looked as non-threatening as Sally. The sight of two strange men would probably cause her to panic and that was the last thing Fowler wanted.

Fowler and Kendal hung back while Sally rapped on the door. It creaked open slightly. It wasn't locked. Sally threw Fowler a look over her shoulder. He nodded even as he was taking his revolver from its holster. Kendal already had his gun out. Sally pushed the door wide open and stepped aside as Fowler and Kendal smoothly entered the apartment, swinging their guns back and forth easily, covering the living room. But there was nothing to cover.

The apartment looked as if someone had stampeded cattle through it.

Chairs were overturned and ripped apart. Books had been taken from the bookshelf and torn apart. So were the bookshelves. Holes had even been knocked in the walls. Sally walked rapidly to the rear of the apartment to check out the bedroom and bathroom, a .25 silver pearl-handled automatic in her hand.

"Damn," Kendal put away his gun, surveyed the carnage. "You think whoever did this was looking for that key we found, Dan?"

"They were looking for something, that's for sure." Fowler looked through the debris on the floor until he found what he was looking for: the telephone. He jiggled the receiver. "Operator. Operator, please."

"Who are you calling?" Kendal wanted to know.

"The police. See if I can get a couple of squad cars out to the Wheeler place."

"You think whoever did this went there?"

"Wouldn't you? They didn't find the key because we have it. So that means they're going to keep looking until they find it." Fowler threw down the phone in disgust. "It's dead. Sally!"

She emerged from the rear of the apartment. "It looks the same back there. Everything's ripped to shreds. Dan, what the hell is going on?"

Fowler motioned for his partners to follow him. "I'll bring you up to speed on the way. Larry, get us to Brooklyn as fast as you can!"

Kendal used the siren all the way from Manhattan, across the bridge into Brooklyn and continued on Flatbush Avenue, pushing the big sedan as fast as it could go, the powerful engine thrumming with power as if the car itself relished being able to rocket through the nighttime streets as such velocity. They picked up several squad cars along the way and Fowler apprised them of the situation via the sedan's radio, advising them to hang back, cut their sirens and let the three agents take the point once they arrived at the Wheeler house. If the police officers heard gunshots they were to move in but not before.

The Wheeler house was a three story brownstone located on Ocean Avenue. Kendal killed the headlights two blocks away from the address and the sedan glided down the wide, dark street like a long shadow. Fowler pointed silently. Kendal and Sally could see several forms being dragged from the brownstone, struggling against the strong hands of the men who were dragging them to a parked truck.

"Hit it, Larry!" Fowler ordered. Kendal cut the headlights on full, the brilliant white light illuminating the truck, the street, the Wheelers and their would be abductors. Fowler saw that the killer Rome was standing

"Fowler…leaned forward and kissed her…"

inside the truck, snarling in rage as he lifted up his Mauser. "Sally, be careful! That guy in the truck-"

Too late, Sally had already bailed out of the back seat and was taking cover behind a parked car, snapping off shots from her automatic. Fowler also bailed out.

Kendal tromped on the pedal and the big sedan leaped forward as if kicked by a giant. The sedan was a virtual fortress on wheels. Armor plated from the hood ornament to the rear bumper. When it hit something, especially a human body, it tended to make a mess. The sedan hit one of the kidnappers and he was thrown a good twenty feet to end up as a bloody smear on the pavement.

Another man was down, holding onto his neck, blood gushing between his fingers. Sally had accurately placed a bullet there.

Rome had climbed into the driver's seat of the truck and had gotten it started. The truck lurched into motion but by then Fowler had reached it. His strong hands seized a handhold on the side of the truck and he swung himself aboard.

Rome turned in his seat, cursing in an obscure dialect that sounded vaguely Chinese to Fowler's ears but also seemed to have element of Arabic as well. Rome got off a shot from his Mauser and Fowler felt the poisoned bullet whiz by his cheek. The last thing Rome would expect Fowler to do was to go on the offensive and that's exactly what he did, launching himself right at the killer.

Fowler's arm batted Rome's gun hand to the side and another bullet shattered the passenger side window. Fowler's short but strong uppercut rocked Rome's head back and forth. Rome bared his teeth, snapping at Fowler's face. Fowler jerked back, one hand holding onto Rome's gun hand while his other hand laid hold of the steering wheel and yanked hard.

The speeding truck screeched, skewed wildly to the right and slammed into several parked cars. Fowler and Rome were thrown about into the truck as it tipped over and crashed on its right side. Rome scrambled for the rear of the truck, seeking to escape.

Fowler tackled him and they both rolled out onto the street. Fowler stood up, yanking the killer to his feet. "You've got some talking to do, mister! Why'd you kill Butterfield? What does the Hip Ling Tong have to do with this?"

Rome laughed, an unpleasant hyena's bark. "You'll find out, Fowler. The Hip Ling knows about you. And they have plans that you should know about *them*!"

And then, incredibly, Rome reached up, laid hold of his own chin and the back of his head and twisted sharply. The breaking of his neck was incredibly loud in the ears of a totally startled Dan Fowler who stood there in open-mouthed amazement, still holding onto the suit lapels of the now limp body, the head lolling in grisly fashion.

Kendal and Sally came running up. "Good God," Kendal said, just as flabbergasted as Fowler. "Did I see what I thought I saw?"

Fowler let the body go and it thumped to the street. "You did. He broke his own neck." Fowler looked down at the body grimly. "And from what he said, I don't think we've seen the last of the Hip Ling Tong, Larry."

The Wheeler house had been searched and secured. No other intruders had been found. Sandra Wheeler sat in the living room with her parents, who were holding onto each other with fierce passion. Sandra looked up with frightened eyes that were nearly blood-red from the crying she had been doing as Fowler entered the living room, taking off his hat.

"Miss Wheeler? I'm Inspector Dan Fowler with the FBI. This is Inspector Kendal and Special Agent Vane. I appreciate the ordeal you've been through but it's vital that I ask you some questions that I very badly need the answers to."

"Brent said that you would probably be the one they'd send." Sandra said with a half-sob.

Fowler, Sally and Kendal swapped astonished looks. Fowler turned back to the young woman and said, "You *knew* that Butterfield was actually Brent Coleman? You knew he was an undercover FBI agent?"

Sandra nodded vigorously in the affirmative. "We were going to be married. Brent told me everything. He said that he was going to resign. We were going to move to some small town in California where nobody knew either one of us and where Brent would be sure he wouldn't run into any crooks he knew." This time Sandra's sob was louder. "We had such plans… we were going to be married…"

Sally went to sit down next to her and wrapped an arm around Sandra's shoulders. Sandra buried her head in Sally's neck and let loose with a storm of tears. Sally looked up at Fowler, intending to ask that he put off the questioning until later. The look on Fowler's face changed her mind. Instead, she pulled back and gave Sandra a shake. "Sandra, you've got to pull yourself together for a few more minutes. Please. We've got to know why Brent was killed."

Kendal stepped forward and gallantly handed Sandra his handkerchief. She wiped her eyes dry and blew her nose before talking. "Brent said he had stumbled on something by accident but it was big. So big that he couldn't resign until he had passed it on to his superiors."

"Do you know what it was?"

"No. But here-" Sandra removed a thin gold chain from around her neck. Hanging from the chain was a key that was a duplicate of the one Fowler had found in Coleman/Butterfield's suite. "Brent gave me this key and said that if anything happened to him I was to give it to whatever agent the Bureau sent."

"What's it for?"

"A safety deposit box. There's a bank in Manhattan. Consolidated Savings and Loan on 10th and 6th. That's where Brent placed whatever it was that got him killed. I hope it's worth it to you." And once again she buried her head in Sally's neck and unleashed a torrent. Mrs. Wheeler moved over to help Sally comfort her daughter.

Mr. Wheeler waved at Fowler. "Go on and do your job, son. We'll be fine."

"Special Agent Vane will stay with you, sir. And I'll have police officers stationed outside until we secure whatever is in that safety deposit box." Fowler shook Mr. Wheeler's hand. "Once we have it in our custody you and your family should be safe. The tong won't have any reason to bother you." Fowler motioned to Kendal. "Let's go."

"Dan, it's the middle of the night! You think you're going to get that bank open now?"

"You're damned right I will. If I have to blow it open with nitro myself. That girl back there deserves to know why the man she loved got killed and Brent Coleman's name needs to be cleared. Whatever is in the safety deposit box will solve this mystery and accomplish both ends."

Kendal nodded. "Yeah, as usual, you're right." Kendal looked over his shoulder at the grieving girl. "Y'know, Dan…I wish I'd known Coleman."

Fowler's face was as unemotional as granite but his voice was soft and compassionate as he replied; "Me too, Larry. Me too."

Washington, DC
Department of Justice Building
One Day Later

The Director closed the Butterfield/Coleman file and looked up at Dan Fowler. "Incredible, Fowler. Simply incredible."

Fowler lit up a cigarette and blew out smoke before answering. "I agree. We'll never know how Coleman got his hands on those counterfeit Chinese bank notes plates. I myself suspected he had many informants, all of who were feeding him information and he stumbled onto the fact that these plates were being made by the tongs operating here in America. He then intercepted the plates and hid them away, no doubt his intention being to pass them onto you. But the tongs put their assassin Rome and his poisoned bullets onto him before he could do so."

The Director shook his head sadly. "I wish to God he'd let me in on what he was doing. I'd have sent you and Kendal to bring him and the plates out safely."

"Don't blame yourself, Director. Coleman was used to operating on his own for so long he figured he could handle this as well. And I'm thinking that he wanted to bring this to you himself. Call it his going away present to you before resigning."

"I told Brent when he started the job that anytime he wanted to walk away it would be fine with me."

"He didn't want to let you down, sir." Fowler said quietly. "I know how he must have felt. None of us ever want to let you down."

"You certainly didn't. I can't thank you enough for what you've done. Brent Coleman will be buried with full honors. Both The Attorney General and I will be speaking at the service. We want to be sure that everybody understands what a contribution Brent made toward preserving international relations between America and China. If the tongs had pulled off flooding the country with counterfeit bank notes it would have eventually caused considerable financial chaos. Our experts tell me that those plates were so good that they were virtually indistinguishable from the real thing."

"Sir? I'd like to bring Miss Wheeler to the funeral."

"Of course. I wouldn't have it any other way. She'll sit with me and The Attorney General." The Director sighed. "And what about this damned tong? The Hip Lings?"

Fowler's voice was cold and hard as he replied; "This is my second run-in with them, Director. I'm certain there's going to be a third. From what Rome told me before he killed himself, The Hip Lings have an interest in me. And after this case I most certainly have an interest in *them*."

"Well, you be careful. I've got a lot more work for you to do."

Fowler stood up, crushed out his cigarette in a round black ashtray and picked up his fedora from The Director's desk. "If that's all, Director?"

"Yes. You're dismissed. Take a couple of days off. You've earned them."

Dan Fowler walked over to the door and placed his hat firmly on his head before saying; "With all due respect, Mr. Director…America's enemies don't take days off."

And with that he opened the door and was striding out of the office with firm, determined steps, eager for a new assignment that he knew would not be long in coming.

The End

Writing "The Undercover Puzzle"

The writing of "The Undercover Puzzle" was in many ways a challenge to me as a writer. Outside of some fan fiction I've written I've mostly written characters that I've created. Dan Fowler was a character I'd never heard of before joining the Airship 27 crowd but he was a character I felt I knew. Strong, capable, confident, principled.

I've always been a fan of those Warner Brothers/RKO crime thrillers of the 1930's, especially the series: Philo Vance, Torchy Blane, The Saint, The Falcon, Mr. Moto, The Lone Wolf, The Crime Doctor…you get the idea. Most of them were quickies cranked out and meant to be disposable entertainment. But I found a lot of 'em quite a lot of fun. I saw my Dan Fowler story as an opportunity to write a sort of homage to those movies. As well as tell a more "realistic" type of story. Most of the stuff I write has several fantastic elements swirling around in the mix but with "The Undercover Puzzle" I wanted to tell a more or less straight ahead crime thriller and save the fantastic elements for other stories and characters.

It's also great to write about cops and federal agents in those days before Miranda when the conflict between the law and the lawless was more like open warfare. Neither side played by the rules and it interests me to write about a guy like Dan Fowler who even though he can fight as dirty as the men he's hunting down makes a conscious choice not to.

Much like removing a bandaid I suppose the best way to get through this is to rip it off as quickly as possible, accept the pain and move on:

My name is DERRICK FERGUSON and I'm from Brooklyn, New York where I've lived most of my life. Married for 25 years to the wonderful Patricia Cabbagestalk-Ferguson who lets me get away with far more than is good for me.

My interests include old radio shows, classic pulps from the 30's/40's, comic books, fan fiction, Star Trek, pop culture, science fiction, animation, television and movies…oh yeah…*movies*. I'm currently the co-host of the podcast **BETTER IN THE DARK** http://betterinthedark.podomatic.com

where my partner Thomas Deja and I rant and rave about movies on a bi-weekly basis.

My primary love is reading and writing and I've written four books to date: ***Dillon And The Voice of Odin***, my love letter to classic pulp action/adventure with a modern flavor. ***Derrick Ferguson's Movie Review Notebook*** and its sequel ***The Return of Derrick Ferguson's Movie Review Notebook***.

Diamondback Vol I: It Seemed Like A Good Idea At The Time, is a spaghetti western disguised as a modern day gangster/crime thriller. For information on how to purchase them, please visit the Pulpwork Press website: http://www.freewebs.com/pulpworkpress/

Anything else you'd like to know about me, check out my Live Journal: http://dferguson.livejournal.com/

in

"Monkey Business"

by
Aaron Smith

A thick plume of smoke rose, from the thick Cuban cigar into the Philadelphia night air, as the Polish gangster walked out the front door of his favorite nightclub. He was a big, heavy man with a face that could turn instantly from a threatening scowl to a jolly Santa Claus-like laugh. He was dressed in an expensive silk suit with a slightly tilted fedora. He walked with supreme confidence, going without bodyguards, secure in his feeling that no one would dare try to do anything to him there on his home turf.

His name was Smokey Wawelski, and he was on top of the world. Born in Krakow in 1893, Wawelski had come to the United States with his father several years later. The old man had been heartbroken when his wife had died of influenza and could not bear to stay in their homeland without her, so he had elected to raise his son in America. They had arrived by way of Ellis Island and then travelled to Pittsburgh, where the father had taken a job in a steel mill. The son, who had been named Stanislaw at birth, grew up watching his father come home every night, back aching, dead tired, with just enough money to scrape by with the rent and a meager amount of food on the table. By the time Stanislaw was twelve, he could stand it no longer. He vowed to find a way to have a better life. He felt the old man would be better off with only one mouth to feed, and so he ran away from home. Sneaking onto a freight train, he soon found himself in Philadelphia, a bigger, cleaner city than Pittsburgh. Stanislaw was a smart boy and could communicate fluently in both Polish and English. He was also a sneaky young man, with an inner willingness to do whatever it took to survive. He taught himself how to pick pockets, and then graduated to stealing cars. He worked his way into one of the city's Irish gangs by claiming that his name was O'Malley. He spent his next decade working his way up through the Irish ranks, but he had a side project going on as well. When not posing as O'Malley, he made numerous contacts in Philadelphia's Polish community, slowly building up his own gang.

By the time he was thirty, he had a large following of thieves, extortionists, arsonists, forgers and even cold-blooded killers. He vanished from the company of his Irish allies and went to work with what he had built in secret. He had made Philadelphia's Polish gangs as much a force to be reckoned with as the Irish or the Italians. The dough started to roll in and he finally felt he had made something of himself. He dressed well, drove an expensive car, and consumed ten Cuban cigars a day. Young Stanislaw had grown up to be Smokey Wawelski, one of the most feared men in Philadelphia.

Wawelski was one of those rare gangsters who seemed to lead a charmed life; he ruled over his territory with an iron fist, the police could never seem to pin anything on him; he was a great success in all his criminal endeavors. At most times, he felt untouchable. This was one such night. He had had dinner at his favorite club, discussed plans with some of his lieutenants, danced with a gorgeous brunette, and was now headed home for the evening. He left the club, getting into his expensive black sedan. He could have easily afforded a chauffer, but preferred to drive himself around, enjoying the feeling of controlling the movements of the vehicle with his own two hands. He drove for twenty minutes, parked in his usual spot, the one no one else would dare to occupy, and left the car to go up to his expensive seventh story apartment.

Once inside, Wawelski went about his usual evening routine. He was proud of his success in life, proud of the fact that he could afford things his father never could, even if he had acquired them through ruthlessness and treachery. His apartment was finely furnished and his attire expensive. He doffed his hat and jacket, donned his red velvet smoking jacket, poured a glass of vodka, sat down, and lit his final cigar of the day. He sipped his drink and smoked, his eyes closed as he carefully considered his next plans to expand his ever-growing empire of crime. He truly was one of the most powerful men in Philadelphia, criminal or legitimate businessman.

He had grown quite relaxed when the silence was abruptly broken by the strangest, most unsettling laughter he had ever heard in his life. It was a terrible sound, an obscene mocking chattering, and a laugh that immediately struck him as being hideously apelike in nature!

The glass tumbled from Wawelski's grip; the clear liquor wet the carpet. The Polish mob boss stood and turned to face the source of the terrible cackling sound. He gasped as he saw the strange figure standing there, leering at him. Wawelski's mind struggled to interpret what he saw, but all he could seem to make of it, in his sudden confusion, was that he was facing a six foot tall monkey, a hairy-faced and wiry limbed beast…dressed in a three-piece suit and round-rimmed bowler hat!

Wawelski froze, so shocked by what he saw that he had no idea how to react. He just stood there. To his further amazement, the well-dressed apelike figure opened its grotesque mouth and actually spoke.

"Hello, Stanislaw."

The monkey spoke…and the monkey leaped forward. As it moved, the bowler hat fell from its head, giving Wawelski an even clearer view of the furry, wild-haired head and the twisted face, teeth bared. It crashed into Wawelski and sent him reeling backwards, straight into the wide window that overlooked the street below. The window broke, shards of glass raining down onto the Philadelphia pavement…followed by the two-hundred and fifty pound body of the Polish gangster! The impact was brutal. Bones snapped, the body broke, and the apelike thing looked down from above, actually smiling at the results of what it had done.

On the sidewalk, Smokey Wawelski was still alive, just barely. He could not move, save for his right hand. He knew he was dying, could see the end coming quickly. Fighting through the pain, the sheer agony of his shattered frame, he dipped his finger in his own blood and reached up to touch the white-painted trash can that stood beside him. With that finger and that blood, he scrawled one word, a word that came from his native language. That word reflected his final living thought. Within seconds, Smokey Wawelski was dead.

An hour later, Detective Carl Drummond of the Philadelphia Police Department's homicide division stood staring down at the corpse of Smokey Wawelski. Rail-thin, bespectacled, and gray-haired, Drummond had been on the force for many years and he was nearing retirement age, but his mind was still as razor-sharp as it had ever been. His younger partner, Detective Goldberg, was unused to seeing such severely shattered bodies, and so his voice quivered slightly as he spoke.

"Do you think it was a suicide, Drummond?"

The elder detective answered with a hint of annoyance in his voice.

"No, Goldberg, I most certainly do not think this was a suicide! First of all, when a man wishes to end his own life, he most likely would throw himself out the window…not through it! Secondly, there was no suicide note. True, there's not always a note, but if Wawelski had wanted to tell us something, he would have written it beforehand, not scrawled it in blood with his dying breath! I wonder what this word means. It must be Polish. Make yourself useful, Goldberg. See if there's a Polish cop around in this crowd; one who speaks the language."

Goldberg turned towards the dozen or so uniformed officers who were busy keeping the reporters and cameramen away from the body. Drummond crouched down to get a closer look at the body and the strange, single word message the dead man had left behind. He stared at the side of the trash can. The blood had run slightly before congealing enough to stick, but the word was clear enough. It said "Moupka."

Minutes later, Goldberg returned to Drummond's side with a uniformed cop.

"Detective Drummond, this is Officer Wysocki. He speaks Polish. Wysocki, can you tell us what that word means?" said Goldberg, pointing to the bloody letters on the trash can.

The young officer bent down to look at the word. "Moupka," he whispered to himself. "Yes, Sir; 'Moupka' is Polish for Monkey!"

"Monkey," Carl Drummond blurted out, surprised. "So Wawelski falls through a glass window, drops seven stories, gets smashed and shattered on the sidewalk, and writes 'monkey' as he dies? Why? Why?"

Officer Wysocki shrugged his shoulders. It made no more sense to him than it made to the two detectives. The body of Smokey Wawelski was soon carted off to the morgue. Gradually, the police and the reporters drifted away from the gruesome scene. Drummond and Goldberg made their way upstairs to Wawelski's apartment. They examined the scene as the midnight breeze blew in through the opening left by the breaking of the large window.

"No obvious signs of a struggle," observed Drummond. "If somebody did push Wawelski through the window, it was either somebody he knew and didn't expect would do such a thing…or he was taken completely by surprise. Wawelski was a big man; I can't imagine he wouldn't have put up a pretty good fight!"

Two weeks later, Drummond and Goldberg sat in the offices of the homicide division. There had been no solid leads in the investigation of Wawelski's death. There had been no witnesses other than those who had run outside after hearing the sound of the body and the broken glass falling to the street. No stool pigeons had offered any information to the detectives. They had nothing. Wawelski's sudden demise remained a mystery.

More disturbing than the lack of leads in the case however, was a certain change in the city of Philadelphia that Carl Drummond had begun to notice. Although Detective Drummond strongly disapproved of any criminal activity and had tried his best to find evidence to bring Smokey Wawelski to justice, he had been glad of one thing during the long span of Wawelski's reign as the city's preeminent mob boss; he had been happy to notice that Wawelski, at least as far as criminals do, had some sort of a sense of honor. Wawelski had, in his employ, thieves, extortionists, arsonists, kidnappers, and even murderers, but innocent blood was almost never spilled as a result of the operations of his empire. There were holdups and robberies, but the victims, although traumatized by the ordeal, were usually left alive. When arson was committed, it was usually on empty buildings late at night. There were killings, but usually of informants or rivals, never of honest citizens. For all Wawelski's criminal acts, he seemed to keep his minions from crossing certain lines. For that, Carl Drummond had always been grateful.

What worried Drummond and Goldberg was that, in the two weeks since Wawelski's death, crime in Philadelphia had taken a turn for the worse; it had grown uglier, more violent, and increasingly brutal. An elderly shop proprietor had been gunned down, riddled with bullets even after voluntarily surrendering all the cash in his till. Several young women had been savagely raped, one beaten severely enough that she had died. The mayor had even received a death threat, although no attempt at assassination had been carried out yet. These were ugly crimes, things that would have never occurred when Smokey Wawelski had been running the Philadelphia mob.

In addition to the increased savagery of the city's criminal elements, Drummond and Goldberg had been unable to ascertain who had taken Wawelski's place as the top man in the organization. The identity of whoever was now running the show seemed to be a closely guarded secret. Why, wondered Carl Drummond? Who was the new face behind the curtains of the underworld, and what connection did this mystery man have to Wawelski and his gruesome, deadly plunge from that seventh story window?

Miles away from the police precinct where Detective Drummond sat pondering the events of the last two weeks, a beat-up black car was speeding towards the outskirts of the city, it's two occupants trying their best to get out of Philadelphia before it was too late. Both the driver and the passenger were hardened criminals, but they had been loyal members of Smokey Wawelski's mob. They may have been crooks, but the sudden shift towards brutality in Philadelphia's underworld had been too much for them. They would not work for the man, if he could even be considered a man, who had taken Wawelski's place. They knew that simply refusing to continue their activities was not an option. All that was left for them to do was to get out of town, and they knew they had to do so as quickly as possible.

They sped along the road that ran out of the city into the more rural areas to its west. Passing out of the city's borders, they both breathed a sigh of relief, but their good feeling was short lived. A shot rang out! The driver struggled to maintain control of the car as it swerved off the road! With a sudden crashing sound, the car slammed into a tree, its journey at an end. The two men opened their doors, began to step out of the vehicle, and were promptly mowed down by two more shots, in quick succession, one bullet for each of their brains! The bodies fell to the grassy ground, both dead before what was happening could even register in their minds! From the wooded area just across the road, the chilling sound of apelike laughter pierced the air.

Back in the city, Carl Drummond had made up his mind. There were still no clues in Wawelski's death, and the string of violent crimes that had begun when Wawelski had fallen continued. The Philadelphia police seemed unable to crack either case; who killed Wawelski, and who had replaced him as boss of the city's most powerful syndicate? Drummond had decided that perhaps the only good option left was to bring a fresh mind and a fresh pair of eyes into the case. He did not bother to consult his superiors, he did not stop to consider asking for permission; he picked up the telephone from his desk and he made a call to Washington, D.C.

"You wanted to see me, Chief?" asked Inspector Dan Fowler of the Federal Bureau of Investigation as he settled into the chair across the desk from his superior. The tough looking, militarily groomed Chief looked back at Fowler with his usual expression of absolute seriousness.

"I did, Fowler. Reports from the medical staff tell me you've recovered fully from the injuries you received at the conclusion of that affair involving the Chinese musician. It's time you got out into the field again. I had an interesting call from an old friend this morning.

"Detective Carl Drummond of the Philadelphia Police Department is an old associate of mine. He called me this morning to tell me about a case that's come his way. He asked if I had a man to send to help him look into certain things that have been happening in the so-called 'City of Brotherly Love.' Now keep in mind, Agent Fowler, that Drummond has not officially requested the assistance of the Bureau, so keep this quiet and don't go barging in questioning the local cops. I want you to go to Philadelphia and quietly...I repeat, quietly...make contact with Drummond and get the scoop on whatever it is that's troubling him. I don't have all the details, but it seems some gang boss out there was assassinated and now whoever's taken his place is wreaking a lot of havoc in some ugly ways. As I said, I've known Carl Drummond for a long time and if he's puzzled, there must be something to whatever's going on there. Get there as soon as you can and give him a hand."

Fowler, who had taken out a cigarette, nodded as he lit it. "It sounds simple enough, chief. Can I take Kendal with me?" he asked, referring to Agent Larry Kendal, his frequent partner on his cases.

The Chief shook his head. "Not this time, Fowler. I've just handed Kendal another assignment. I can't have two of my agents running off to Philadelphia on an 'unofficial' case. You'll have to take this one alone."

Dan Fowler had grown quite used to being given sudden travel plans by the Chief. He always had a suitcase packed and ready to go in the trunk of his car. He didn't even bother to go back to his apartment. He left the Chief's office in the Department of Justice Building, and headed straight to the airport. A few hours later, the plane landed in Philadelphia and Fowler disembarked. He made his way to the downtown part of the city and quickly located the small diner where the Chief had told him that Detective Carl Drummond would rendezvous with him.

It was early afternoon when Fowler entered *The Unwashed Pot*. He'd have a hard time thinking of a more unappetizing name for a diner, he thought to himself as he walked through the front door. The interior was not full by any means. There were three men in what looked like mechanics' coveralls sitting at the counter, apparently on their lunch breaks. There was one very fat waitress scurrying, walrus-like, from area to area, refilling coffee cups and taking orders from the few other patrons scattered about the place. Fowler knew Carl Drummond as soon as he saw him. He was the only person in the place who even remotely resembled a cop. Fowler sat down in the booth with Drummond, who had already consumed half a cup of coffee.

Drummond extended his hand to shake Fowler's.

"Thanks for coming, Agent Fowler." He handed a large envelope to Fowler. "This is the file on Wawelski, the man who was killed. Look it over when you have a chance. I spent years trying to find a way to connect Smokey Wawelski to the crimes that I knew he was responsible for…but he seemed to have a knack for leaving very little, if any, evidence behind, and he seemed to have taught this skill to his underlings too. I suppose that's all irrelevant now, as the man is dead. Somebody else, possibly, and I'm tempted to say probably, the man who killed him has taken his place. The problem is, Agent Fowler, I can't seem to get anywhere in sorting this mess out…and I have suspicions that the rest of the department isn't exactly doing its best to crack this case either. That's why I asked your boss for a little favor, for a man to take a fresh look at the situation, working from outside the police force."

"That's understood, Detective Drummond," said Fowler. "I'll do whatever I can to help. By the way, how do you know the Chief anyway? No offence, but you're about twenty years older than he is, so I'm curious."

Drummond laughed. "No offense taken, Agent; I'm perfectly aware of how old I am! Your Chief and I were partners in the Bureau about twenty years ago! Back then, he was the junior partner…if you can imagine that! I taught him everything he knows, but he'd never admit that to you or me or anybody else."

"Interesting," said Fowler. "Why'd you leave the Bureau, if you don't mind the question?"

"Well, son, where were you three hours ago?" asked Drummond.

"Washington," was Fowler's reply.

"And where are you now?" Drummond asked next.

"Philadelphia," said Fowler, starting to wonder why his question was being answered with questions.

"That is why I left the Bureau!" said Drummond. "I got sick of airplanes and trains and boats and being in motion more than I was still, of being on the road or in the air more than I was home. I wanted to stay in one place for awhile, but still do the work of an investigator. So, one night I was in my office at the Bureau and I decided to just go somewhere else. I had a big map of the United States on my office wall. I stood across the room from that map and I picked up a dart. Then I closed my eyes and I threw that dart in the direction of that map, telling myself I'd go to whatever big city that dart came closest to. Well, I hit Philly, and here I am now!

"You'll find my home number and address and office number in that envelope. Call me if you need me, but don't let the department know you're here. I don't want it becoming known that I've asked the FBI for help. I'll let you investigate however you see fit. Good luck, Agent Fowler, and thank you."

Carl Drummond got up and left the diner. Fowler sat and finished his coffee as he opened the file and began to read.

Halfway across Philadelphia from the diner that Dan Fowler was just leaving; three men were gathered together in a small office on the second floor of a typical city building. Two of them were casually dressed in slacks, shirt and ties. They were former members of Smokey Wawelski's mob who had chosen to continue their work under a new leader. The third man was their new leader. He was tall and thin, dressed in a more expensive suit. His face could not be seen, as it was wrapped in a scarf, with a bowler hat pulled down over the forehead.

The scarf-headed man spoke, in a Polish accent, as the others listened.

"Those men, who, like yourselves, have chosen to remain here and work for me, shall be suitably rewarded for work well done. I am not my predecessor, as you should have realized by now. Crime is a serious business, not to be tempered by mercy or decency. The weaknesses of Stanislaw Wawelski are not to continue under my command. When there is work to be done, it shall be done completely. There is to be no so-called honor, no weakness, and no hesitation. By fulfilling my orders to the letter, you will see the fruits of our labors increased accordingly. I have a job for the two of you. There is one man, among all the police force of this city, who seems to be quite adamant in his will to put a stop to our activities. This can be tolerated no longer. You both know of whom I speak, and I trust that you will deal with him accordingly. Now go!"

The two men left immediately, knowing that their new master was not to be disappointed.

After the diner, Dan Fowler had gone to rent a room at a nice, but not overly expensive, hotel. He could have afforded a fancier room with his FBI expense account, but he saw no need for extra luxuries as he would probably not be spending much time in the room anyway. He opened the room's curtains to let in the late afternoon sunlight and sat by the window to finish reading the police file on the dead mob boss. The file turned out to contain a lot of guesses and suspicions about just how far Wawelski's reach had extended into the criminal underworld of Philadelphia, but it also demonstrated just how little concrete evidence had ever been found against the man. The only thing of real potential use to Fowler seemed to be the names and addresses of several people who were suspected of being closely associated with Wawelski's gangs. Fowler decided that those associates would be the people to begin the investigation with. Once he had finished with the file, he took out a map of the city that he had bought at the airport. He opened the map, spreading it out on the room's bed, and stared at it for nearly an hour, his mind and his photographic memory, sharpened by years of training, committing the layout of the city and the locations and intersections of its main streets to memory. Fowler was used to traveling to different parts of the United States on each case to which he was assigned, and he had learned many tricks to learning about each new town as quickly as humanly possible. When he was satisfied that he knew enough about both Wawelski and the city in which he now was, he decided to call Detective Drummond and let him know his plans to begin his work. He glanced at his watch. It was now past six o'clock. He didn't know how late Drummond usually worked, so he decided to call him at home first. He picked up the room's telephone and was soon connected. He heard Drummond's phone ring once, then twice.

The phone was picked up on the other end. "Hello," said a raspy voice with a hint of a European accent. Fowler immediately knew that it was not the aging detective.

"Drummond, is that you?" Fowler asked, knowing it wasn't.

"I'm sorry," said the voice on the phone, "Detective Drummond can't talk to you at this time. He's busy dying."

The line clicked off. Fowler slammed down the phone, and then picked it up again. He had the operator connect him to the police department.

"Get some men to the home of Detective Carl Drummond," Fowler barked at the desk sergeant who had answered. "Get them there now!" He reached for the file that Drummond had given him, and found the address that had been written on it under Drummond's number.

By the time Fowler arrived at Drummond's residence, it was all over. There were detectives and uniformed officers all over the lawn and front steps. A few reporters milled about the area too. The coroner's van was just leaving the scene. Fowler didn't bother to try to go in to look around. He had promised the detective that he wouldn't announce his presence to the rest of the police force, and he wasn't about to break that promise because of the man's death. He told his cab driver to take him back to his hotel. He knew he had to call the Chief, and he dreaded being the bearer of this terrible news.

"Dammit!" was the only word the Chief spoke at first when Fowler had told him, over the telephone, of the unfortunate fate of Carl Drummond. After that one word, the line went silent for several long moments. Fowler did not say anything; he just waited, knowing that the Chief was not a man who often allowed his emotions to show. Finally, the bureau's commander began to speak again, this time in slow, deliberate syllables. Fowler could tell that the Chief was using his iron will to keep his voice from cracking with grief.

"Fowler, if I know you as well as I think you do, you asked Carl how he and I knew each other, and he probably told you, so you know how long he

"His face could not be seen…"

and I were friends. There was a time when he was a mentor…a father to me. Listen, Fowler. This is what you're going to do. Don't bother with the police there in Philadelphia. From what I've heard, not many of them are worth their weight in sawdust, let alone anything else. Drummond was, but he's gone. Never mind the cops there; you're working for me! I want you to find out who did this, and I want you to find out who that person is working for too. Find out who killed Carl, and find out who ordered the hit…and take them down! Use whatever means necessary. I want those people…dead or alive. Do what you have to do, and I promise you you'll have the full support of the bureau in this matter."

That was all that was said. The Chief hung up. That was all that Dan Fowler needed to hear. He put the phone down. He put on his shoulder holster after checking his gun to be sure it was loaded. He pulled on his jacket to conceal it. It was warm enough in Philadelphia, being only early in the autumn, that he had no need for a coat over his suit. He took a list of names and addresses he had copied from the file on Smokey Wawelski. He grabbed his fedora. All that he needed on his person, he walked quickly out of his room, down the stairs, choosing not to wait for the elevator, through the hotel lobby, and out the front door onto the evening streets of Philadelphia. Special Agent Fowler was ready to get to work, and he would not stop until his case was closed.

The first stop on Fowler's list was a bar called *The Declaration of Intoxication*, obviously a bad play on words referring to the most famous political document to be signed in the city of Philadelphia. According to the file that Drummond had given Fowler, this bar was a crossroads of sorts, a place where those who had prominent positions in all factions of Philadelphia's underworld could gather. It was also considered a neutral zone, an establishment where there was an unspoken agreement that no member of one gang would attack or assault a member of another. Deals were made there, discussions took place, truces were made or broken, but violence was not tolerated. Fowler figured he'd go in, sit down, order a drink, and observe and listen, hoping to get lucky and find some hint or clue to what had been happening to change the state of crime in Philadelphia so drastically in such a short time.

Fowler located the bar quickly enough, his crash course in Philadelphia geography making him more knowledgeable than most newcomers to the city. He walked in the front door of the place. He wasn't worried about attracting unwanted attention, for although he was a stranger there, he had spent enough time among criminals in his career that he knew how they talked and acted and he had full confidence in his ability to blend in. As he entered, he glanced around. It was a dark bar, a large place with a multitude of tables where private conversations could be held, and a long bar area with about a dozen stools. The place was incredibly smoky too, to the extent that Fowler, who smoked a pack a day himself, had to stifle the urge to cough a bit on his first breath of the bar's stale air. He walked over to the bar and sat down. The bartender, a hefty bald man with a ridiculous looking handlebar moustache came over.

"What can I get you, buddy?" asked the barman.

"Beer, just beer," Fowler responded, not wanting anything stronger to impair his ability to watch and listen to those around him.

The cold bottle was placed in front of Fowler and he took a big gulp of the bitter brew. The bartender went back to his business, wiping the counter and seeing to the needs of his other customers. It was nearly nine o'clock now and the place was beginning to fill up. Most of those present looked, to Fowler, like typical underworld types, shady characters with dark agendas hidden behind their beady eyes. Most present were men, but a few had walked in with women on their arms, the sort of women who could turn heads, but would probably never wind up as wives.

Fowler continued to watch, slowly sipping his drink, as more and more people filed into the now busy pub. No one bothered him, all of them going about their business. He could see that the bar patrons divided themselves up into groups, separated mostly by ethnicity, as the city had criminal gangs composed of those of Irish, Polish, and Italian descent.

After an hour of discreet observation, Fowler was able to tell who came from what mob, who the bosses were, and who their minions were. When it came to the criminal class, there were definite differences in the ways that men of different ranks and positions conducted themselves. Among those in the bar, Fowler's attention was especially drawn to one man, the sort of man whose presence there seemed incongruous, as if he belonged to a separate category from the rest of those present. He was a small man among the burly tough sort that seemed to compose the rest of the crowd. He had sparse black hair, was clean shaven, and had tiny black mischievous eyes. His features told Fowler that he was Polish, like a good portion of the men in the bar, but he obviously belonged to the group of men whose crimes were guided by their brains rather than their brawn or their guns. He had caught Fowler's attention as a man who might be worth watching. Also odd was the fact that despite his small stature and quiet demeanor, he was accompanied by the two most stunning women in the place, a gorgeous long-legged redhead and a bubbly, giggling blonde. They seemed way out of the little man's league, but their eyes did not wander, and the short accountant-like man had their full attention as the unlikely trio sat and drank.

Fowler decided that he wanted to know who this man was. His investigative instincts had lit the fires of curiosity in his mind. He turned on his barstool and looked straight at the little man, making sure that his gaze was noticed. The little man could not help but see that Fowler was watching him. He stood up from his table. The two women started to rise with him, but a quick motion of his hand ordered them to remain seated and they did. He got up and slowly, confidently walked over to the bar where Fowler waited. The stool beside Fowler was unoccupied, so the man sat down. He eyed Fowler suspiciously, sizing him up, judging him, and then began to speak. His voice had the Polish accent that Fowler had expected. His words came out slowly, deliberately, in a volume that was just above a whisper, lending a strange, hissing, almost serpentine manner to his voice.

"When I first came through the doors, I suspected you of being a policeman…but I think you are not. You have hardness to your face that the lazy policemen of this town do not possess. Still, I think you are a stranger here." The 's' in 'stranger' was oddly elongated, adding to the snakelike aura of the odd little man.

Fowler decided to play along with the assumptions that were being made about him. After all, he was not exactly a policeman, at least not the local kind, and he was, indeed, a stranger to Philadelphia.

"Yes, sir," said Fowler, "I just got into town this morning. I don't really know anybody in these parts, at least until now. Pleased to meet you." He extended his hand. The little man did not shake it.

"I am certain that you know this to be a bar of an abnormal kind," the strange little man said to Fowler. "Would you, perhaps, have come here hoping to find work?"

"Actually," replied the undercover G-Man, with a little bit of sarcasm, "I came here hoping for a beer. But if somebody wanted to offer me work, I'd be willing to hear them out."

"My name," said the little snake-man "is Piotr. If you stay here in Philadelphia for long, you will find that I am a man of some importance in a very influential organization here. Now, my friend, this organization has recently come under new leadership, and some of its older members have elected to part ways with this new leader. This leaves me, as a great helper to this leader, in something of a predicament. I need more men to fulfill certain duties. I am going to ask you three questions. Should you answer yes to them all, then perhaps there is good work for you to do here in Philadelphia."

"All right, friend," said Fowler, "go ahead and ask."

Piotr posed his three questions.

"Have you ever killed a man? Have you ever had to keep a grave secret, under penalty of death should you reveal it to anyone? Are you willing to go to great lengths to accomplish a goal, provided the rewards are adequate?"

Fowler nodded in response to each successive question.

"Good, good," said Piotr. He handed a small card to Fowler; there was something scrawled in tiny, neat handwriting on the back of the card. Fowler did not read it then, but put it away in his pocket. Piotr continued, "Come to this address in the morning. You will learn things then. What is your name?"

Fowler made up an alias on the spot. While his face was unknown to most, due to the Chief doing his best to keep his agents' faces out of the newspapers, his name was a noteworthy one among the circles of the underworld.

"The name is Franklin; Don Franklin"

Piotr stood up from the barstool.

"Very well, Mister Franklin; I shall see you again tomorrow."

He went back to his lady friends. Fowler finished off his beer, tossed some money onto the bar, and got up and left the place. He went back to his hotel to get some sleep, certain that the next day would be an interesting one.

Fowler made it back to his room without incident. He washed, undressed, smoked the day's last cigarette, and climbed into bed. As he always did when sleeping in an unfamiliar city while on a case, he placed his gun under his pillow in easy reach should something occur during the night. He closed his eyes and quickly fell into slumber. The minutes began to tick by, turning into hours as the late evening melted into the early morning. Fowler slept peacefully for most of the time but, finally, something stirred him from his sleep.

There are certain things which set the most successful of Federal agents apart from the merely mediocre men in that profession; certain skills, certain traits. These characteristics include an extraordinary ability to notice the details of one's surroundings. Things that would escape the notice of the ordinary man are part of the entire set of perceptions that come into the awareness of the skilled investigator. Dan Fowler was one such skilled agent. With his sharp eyes, he could see what others missed. With his well-honed sense of hearing, he could detect sounds and words that would otherwise get lost in the wall of noise that surrounds us at most times. Even his senses of smell, taste and touch had been sharpened by experience.

There in the early morning hours, the city of Philadelphia still shrouded in darkness, something made Dan Fowler awake. His eyes opened first, and he did not know why he had come out of his deep sleep, only that there had to have been reasons. His eyes peered straight ahead, but he saw no unexpected movement in the shadows. He strained his ears, listening as hard as he could, but he heard no unusual sounds, only the buzzing of street sounds from outside the hotel windows. He did not move, only observed, uncertain of what had made him stir. Then, he found the answer. He inhaled, sniffing the hotel room's air. There it was; a hint of perfume, a slight scent that did not quite fit in a room occupied by one lone man. Someone else was there; a woman, silent and out of sight, but a woman nonetheless. Of that, Dan Fowler was sure.

Moving carefully, making certain that his sly motion was undetectable; he slid his hand under his pillow and gripped the handle of his gun. Then he moved swiftly, in a blur of carefully choreographed action. The gun in his right hand was instantly aimed straight ahead as his upper body sat up straight in bed, while his left hand pulled the little chain on the bedside lamp, flooding the small room in sudden light.

There she stood, in the perfect aim of Fowler's gun, a tall, slender brunette of about twenty-five, dressed in the sleek black tights and top that marked her as a professional, and quite stunning, cat burglar.

The girl gasped, caught off guard by the speed of Fowler's movements and the sudden illumination of the area. Seeing the gun aimed straight at her breast, her hands shot up instinctively into the air, in the gesture that was universally understood to mean "Don't shoot me!"

Fowler held the gun steady. The girl stared back, wide-eyed and afraid. "I'm not here to rob you! I'm not here to rob you!" she insisted, trying to get her point across before the man with the gun could use his weapon. "I've come to warn you! I'm trying to help!" She spoke clear English, but there was a hint of a Polish accent, as if she had been born in the United States, but raised in an immigrant household. Fowler, his trained observational skills always at work, guessed that her parents had come here from their European homeland, but that she had been born in Philadelphia or, judging by the American portion of her accent, somewhere else on or near the East Coast.

"Warn me about what?" Fowler demanded to know, slowly lowering the gun, but keeping a firm grip on it in case the girl should make a sudden move.

Fowler's unexpected guest seemed to relax a little now that the gun was no longer aimed so threateningly at her. She took in a deep breath and began to answer the question.

"Warn you about that man you were talking with at the bar. Stay away from Piotr; he's bad news! He's a dangerous man! I saw you with him…and I know you're a stranger here…so I followed you here. Enough people have been hurt by his kind in recent weeks. If you know what's good for you… get away from him…and get away from this city!"

Fowler was intrigued by the idea that this woman, obviously a career thief, a criminal, would still have the decency to at least try to warn a complete stranger of danger, even without knowing anything about the character of the one she was trying to warn! For all she had known, entering Fowler's room in the middle of the night could have resulted in her being raped or even killed, yet she had come anyway.

"Sit down," Fowler said, motioning to the chair against the wall across from the bed. "I'm not going to shoot you. Let's talk."

She did as Fowler suggested and sat down in the chair. "I'm sorry if I startled you," she said. "But I couldn't just come up to your floor and knock. If I were to be seen here, it would be unsafe for both of us. There are those who would not approve of our speaking to one another. So…I climbed the outer walls of the hotel and came in through your window."

"Impressive," Fowler remarked. "Now tell me what you came here to supposedly warn me about."

The pretty cat burglar paused for a moment, considering how to best begin her tale. Finally, she began to speak again.

"I know you only just arrived in Philadelphia, but I would assume that by now you have heard the name Wawelski…Smokey Wawelski."

Fowler nodded. "Yes, I have. He was that gangster who took a dive where there wasn't a swimming pool, wasn't he?"

The girl winced. Fowler had phrased that sentence in a sarcastic tone intentionally, fishing for an emotional response from the girl. Her facial expression, features momentarily twisted in grief, told him a good portion of her story without words being necessary. She continued to talk.

"Yes, you could put it crudely like that. But he certainly didn't throw himself out of that window! He was not the type of man who would resort to suicide no matter what! He was murdered!"

Fowler stood up from the bed, walking over to the room's small closet in his shorts and took his clothes out, pulling on his pants as he responded to the girl's short outburst of emotion.

"Look, I'm sorry if that came out wrong. I'm not used to mincing words. I take it you knew him then?"

The girl averted her eyes, in feigned politeness, from the sight of Fowler getting dressed. She stared at the opposite wall as she went on with her speech.

"Yes, I knew him. He was my father…not by blood…but as much a father to me as anyone ever was. My parents were Polish immigrants, I was born here. When I was twelve years old, they died, together, in a fire. The state people came and took me and put me in a government orphanage… but I hated it there! I escaped one night and made my way back to the neighborhood where I grew up…but I had no money, and no place to sleep. I was hungry and cold and alone. I managed to survive for a few weeks by taking scraps of food from restaurant garbage cans. Finally, I decided that

I had to resort to stealing! I taught myself to pick pockets, to climb into unlocked windows, to fit into places that no grown man could get into... but that a skinny little girl could squeeze into quite easily. I found that I was quite talented as a thief and, because it was for survival, I felt no guilt or remorse."

"One evening I saw Wawelski leaving his lawyer's office. I recognized him, knowing him to be well known in town and knowing him to have plenty of money. I decided to try to rob him. I walked up behind him, using my ability to remain unnoticed, and I went for his wallet. That was the first time I was ever caught in the act. He spun around, faster than a man that large should have been able to! He caught me by the wrist and nearly broke my arm! I thought he would kill me...and I started to cry. Something about me, and my desperation, must have reminded him of his own youth...and he took me to get something to eat, and he listened to my story. He took me under his wing, adopted me in every way but officially, and treated me like a daughter, welcoming me into his 'family business,' and teaching me to be an even better thief than I already was. I grew up, from a tiny, starving pickpocket, into the best sneak thief and cat burglar in Philadelphia! I loved that man, my mentor and my adopted parent. Now he's dead...and the one who I believe killed him has twisted everything that he worked so hard to build, twisted it into a brutal monstrosity of murder and chaos! That's why I came to warn you. Don't go to that meeting in the morning! Don't become part of this!"

Fowler knew he had to ask the right questions of this woman. He knew that if she knew as much as she seemed to know, her appearing in his room could be a very convenient shortcut to the completion of his case.

"Who killed Wawelski?" Fowler asked her. "What is his name?"

"I...I don't know his name," she admitted. "No one knows his name... but they're all afraid of him...terrified! He took over the organization and he killed some of Wawelski's top lieutenants, those who wouldn't go along with his takeover. He brought a new ugliness to the underworld of the city, a terrible brutality that was never there before. And nobody knows what he really looks like either. There has to be something wrong with him, some kind of deformity. He wears a thick scarf that hides his face; he never takes it off!"

Fowler was growing frustrated now.

"So you really can't tell me anything, can you?"

She paused, looking at Fowler as if trying to decide if she should say what had come to her mind next. She spoke.

"Listen to me. I can't tell you more, but I've warned you not to get involved with all this. But, I think you're the stubborn type, the type who isn't going to listen to my warnings anyway, so I'm going to make you an offer. I know you still plan to go and meet with Piotr in the morning, but let me explain something. Smokey had more resources than these men who have tried to take his place are aware of. He left a hell of a lot of money stashed away…and I know where it is! It's yours if you want it…if you do something for me! Go ahead and keep your date with Piotr…and when you go there, kill him…and kill the man he works for now! Do that…and the money is yours! It'll be more than he offers you, I guarantee that."

Fowler had had enough of his visitor.

"Lady, you just made a big mistake!" he said. "I'm not who you think I am."

He was fully dressed now and reached into his pocket, taking out his badge. He held it up for her to see.

"You just tried to bribe a Federal agent into becoming a hired killer. That'll get you a nice long stretch in the big house!"

The girl panicked; she bolted for the door, trying to get away now that she felt threatened with arrest. Fowler never gave her the chance to get away. He pounced, lunging forward, grabbing her by the legs and bringing her crashing down to the floor.

She tried to scratch him, to rake her nails across his face, but he grabbed her by the wrist and forced her hand down. He slapped her once, across the face. That was enough to stop her flailing and struggling. She fell still and began to cry, sobbing, weeping.

"All right, all right," Fowler said to her, "no need for the tears. I'm not going to arrest you, at least not now. But you'd better be prepared to help me out. You know things that I'm going to need to know too if I'm going to get to the bottom of what's happening in this town."

He released his hold on her and stood up. She stood as well, backing up against the wall, still trembling and afraid of what Fowler might do next. He reached into his jacket and handed her his card. "Here's my card. You know where I'm staying. Check back in with me when you can; later tonight if possible. If you can't find me here, leave a sealed message for me at the front desk, letting me know how to find you, and when. The name is Fowler; Dan Fowler. Now get out of here. I have an appointment to keep. By the way, you never told me your name."

She laughed, apparently feeling somewhat better about the situation.

"My name; well, the one my parents gave me is unpronounceable by most Americans. Just call me Marie."

With that, she left Fowler's presence, using the door this time.

Fowler did not go back to bed. He sat awake for the rest of the early morning hours, smoking and thinking. He left the hotel at eight-thirty and had his coffee in a nearby diner. At nine o'clock sharp, he made his way to the address that Piotr had given him in the bar the night before. He was not sure what to expect at this meeting, but he was ready, mentally and physically, for anything, and his shoulder-holstered gun was cleaned and loaded.

He found the address easily enough. He entered the front door of a building that looked like it should have housed numerous offices, but seemed to be deserted. There was no one in the lobby. The elevator had an 'out of order' sign on the door, so Fowler looked around until he found the stairs. He made his way up to the fifth floor, walked down the hall and came to an open door. He walked in. The man he knew as Piotr was sitting in a big armchair in a room otherwise devoid of furnishings. On either side of Piotr's chair stood another man. They were big men, both with obviously European features. Fowler knew immediately what they were. They were what men who knew about situations like this one would call 'goons,' henchmen who were paid not for their brains, but for their brawn and their ability and willingness to hit first and ask questions later. Fowler sized them up as quickly as possible, his sharp, experienced mind estimating which was the stronger, which was the weaker, and formulating a strategy that he could easily implement should he have to confront them physically.

Piotr looked up as Fowler came in. He greeted Fowler by the alias that he had been given the night before.

"Good morning, Mr. Franklin. It pleases me to see that you demonstrate punctuality. I assume you have had sufficient time to consider my offer."

Fowler nodded. "Yes, and I'd be glad to take on the work if it pays well. I do have a question though."

"Ask it then, Mr. Franklin," said Piotr.

"Well I don't want you to take offense to this, friend," said Fowler, "but I've been around the block a few times, and you've got 'Yes Man' written all over you in big, bright letters. I'd like to know who I'm really working for."

Piotr scowled for a moment, then resumed his plastic smile and responded to what Fowler had said.

"Mr. Franklin…had the man who employs me wanted to meet you, he would have come here himself, but he did not. You, Mr. Franklin, are one tiny fish in a very large sea. Perhaps someday you will grow up to be a shark, but for now you are a fish. I will give you an assignment, you will complete it, and I will pay you. You will receive five thousand dollars! After that, assuming you do well, perhaps you will be officially welcomed into our organization. On that day, should he see fit, your true employer will grace you with his presence. Until then, you will answer to me. Is that understood?"

Fowler nodded again. "Clear as a bell, Mister. Now what's this little job

"He pounced...grabbing her leg..."

you want me to do?"

Piotr reached into his jacket pocket and took out a photograph. He spoke as he handed it to Fowler. "Take a good look at this face, Franklin. Remember it."

Fowler took the photograph and looked at it. It was Marie, the girl who had broken into his room in the early morning hours! He feigned ignorance of her identity.

"Who is she? Not a bad lookin' dame," he said.

"Her looks are irrelevant!" Piotr snapped. "What matters is that she is a potential enemy of the organization! She calls herself Marie, and she is the adopted daughter of the man who used to run our business. Your task, Mr. Franklin, is to see that she does not live long enough to meddle in our business affairs. Is that understood?"

Fowler handed the picture back and nodded. "Understood, Pete; the girl's as good as dead. I'll be back tomorrow for my pay." He turned and walked out of the room, already formulating a plan to nab Piotr and his boss.

Fowler stopped for lunch, then made a quick stop to pick up a small can of red paint from a small shop near the hotel. Then he returned to his hotel room. He sat down in the room's chair and picked up the telephone, calling the police precinct where Carl Drummond had worked.

"I'm trying to reach the partner of the late Detective Carl Drummond," Fowler said to the officer who had answered the phone. "I'm afraid I don't know his name."

"No problem, buddy," said the desk sergeant. "That would be Detective Goldberg. Hang on for a minute and I'll see if he's available."

Moments later, another voice came on the line.

"Homicide; this is Goldberg speaking."

"Hello, Detective," said Fowler. "We've never met, but my name is Fowler. I'm with the FBI. My boss at the bureau is an old friend of your partner, Drummond. Listen…please don't advertise the fact that I'm in Philadelphia, but I thought you might want in on a shot at avenging your partner's death…and bringing in the men responsible…dead or alive. Okay, Goldberg, here's what I need you to do. Meet me at ten tonight at the Independence Plaza Hotel, room 423. I need you to bring one of those cameras you boys use to photograph crime scenes. Do you think you can manage that? Good, good; I'll see you then Goldberg."

Fowler hung up the telephone and spent the next few hours thinking about what he had planned. He hoped that Marie would show up that night as he had asked her to. His plan would depend on it.

Hours later, Fowler heard a knock on the room's door. He rose and opened the door to find Detective Goldberg standing there. Although Fowler had never seen him before, he immediately knew who he was.

"Come on in, Detective," Fowler said. "We have some catching up to do while we wait for our third party to arrive."

The two men, both eager to bring in the men responsible for Carl Drummond's demise, got acquainted with each other while they waited. Fowler filled Goldberg in on all that had happened so far. An hour later, the knocking on the door began again. Fowler opened the door and admitted Marie to the room.

"You!" shouted Goldberg. "I ought to arrest you right now! Fowler, this woman is the most notorious jewel thief in the city! What is she doing here?"

Fowler stepped in between the overeager policeman and the attractive thief.

"Easy, Detective; this girl's on our side, at least for tonight. Trust me, Goldberg, I'm choosing the far lesser of two evils in this fine city. Now both of you listen to me; here's what we have to do."

Fowler quickly provided Goldberg and Marie with a summary of what had been discussed during his morning meeting with Piotr. Once all present had been filled in on the details, Fowler began giving instructions.

He walked over to Marie, who was wearing a light tan blouse. He took out a pocket knife and slashed a jagged tear in her top. She did not protest, having already been informed about what Fowler had planned. Once the shirt had been sufficiently torn, Fowler took out the little can of red paint he had bought that afternoon and smeared some of the paint onto Marie's clothing, face and neck. He had her lay on the hotel room's floor, mouth open in an expression of shock, eyes slightly open but rolled back in imitation of death. Fowler stepped back and looked down at the gruesome scene he had created. He nodded his approval, and then turned to Detective Goldberg, who had been silently watching the grim spectacle.

"Detective, I hope you have that camera ready. Snap a couple shots of our actress here!"

The small room was soon flooded by flashes of light as the camera recorded the "dead girl" on the carpeted floor.

Morning came again and Dan Fowler was up at the crack of dawn. He smoked the day's first cigarette, dressed, and headed out into the Philadelphia streets. He stopped for breakfast before making his way to the building where he had met with Piotr and his goons on the previous morning. As he entered the building, the first rays of sunlight were beginning to obliterate the darkness of the early morning hours. Fowler made a slight, barely noticeable gesture with his left hand as he went inside. On the street nearby, the gesture was seen only by the person it was intended for, Detective Goldberg, who was hidden from the sight of any pedestrians who might happen to be walking by. A plan had been worked out in Fowler's room the night before, and Goldberg was ready to follow it to the letter.

Fowler made his way upstairs to the room where he knew Piotr would be waiting. Sure enough, he found exactly what he had expected to see. Piotr sat there, exactly as he had the day before, in his chair, one bodyguard on each side. The only discernable difference was the black briefcase that stood on the floor at the Polish gangster's feet.

"Good morning, Mr. Franklin," said the short but gloweringly evil Piotr. "How did you fare on your small but vital task for me?"

Fowler was not in a mood to waste any time. He put on his best thuggish scowl, imitating the facial expressions of the many evil men he had encountered in his time with the FBI, reached into his jacket pocket, and took out the small group of photographs that Goldberg had hurriedly developed for him. He thrust the grisly pictures into Piotr's hand and smiled wickedly.

"Here you go, boss. The bitch is dead."

Piotr smirked with perverse pleasure as he glanced down at what he thought was a real exhibit of doom. "You have done well, my friend," he said. The way he pronounced "friend," the tone of malicious glee in his voice, sent shivers down Fowler's spine, the sort of shivers that a good, honest man feels when he stares into the face of a pure monster.

Piotr kicked the briefcase so that it slid across the floor towards Fowler. The undercover G-Man picked up the case. He opened it, smiling a fake evil smile as he viewed the case's contents; numerous wads of crisp bills, adding up to an amount of five thousand dollars!

Fowler smiled again. This time it was his real smile, a display of emotion that often came to his face when he knew he was close to reaching an objective, to succeeding in a mission. He had seen all he had needed to see, he had what he needed right there in his hands. He let go of the case and it fell to the floor; the money spilled out, fives, tens, twenties and even bigger bills scattering upon the carpet less floor.

"What are you doing?" exclaimed the confused Piotr.

Fowler drew his gun. The goon on the left drew his own pistol. There was no hesitation in Dan Fowler. One quick shot rang out, the bullet made contact, and the tall thug fell backwards to the floor! The second bodyguard advanced, his hand taking a gun from his shoulder holster. He fared no better than his associate, for the door flew open, helped along by a swift kick from Detective Goldberg. The plainclothes sleuth already had his weapon out and the big Polish man was blown away before he could get a shot off!

The two goons lay dead on the floor. Goldberg and Fowler both stood with smoking guns in their hands. Piotr cowered. Apparently, he had trusted his thugs to do his dirty work for him, so he had come to the meeting unarmed. Fowler looked down at the pathetic little criminal.

"My name is not Don Franklin. I'm Special Agent Daniel Fowler of the Federal Bureau of Investigation, and you are under arrest for bribing a federal agent, conspiracy to commit murder, and a whole slew of other things that I'll write down when we're finished here. Goldberg, cuff this little weasel!"

An hour later, Goldberg and Fowler sat at the precinct. They both had freshly brewed, steaming cups of coffee in their hands. Fowler was quite content with the way the morning had gone so far. The Philadelphia police commissioner had been quite angry at Fowler's being in the city without official notification, but a brief call from the Chief had calmed the head cop down considerably. There was still unfinished business left though, and Fowler was not the type of man to rest on his laurels for long before getting back to work.

"Goldberg," said Fowler as he swallowed the last of his hot java, "I'm going into that holding cell to have a word with our new friend. I'll do this alone…and I'll do it my way, but I want you close by in case I get carried away. I don't want to beat him until he can't talk, at least not before he tells me what I want to know."

Fowler entered Piotr's cell. Goldberg locked the door behind him. The mob lieutenant sat on the cot, glaring up at the G-Man. He did not speak first. Fowler took off his jacket and handed it to Goldberg through the bars. He did so slowly, choosing to build suspense in Piotr's mind, a method he had learned through many interrogations during his distinguished career as an agent. He rolled up his shirt sleeves. He took off his fedora and tossed it aside. He took out a cigarette and lit it, inhaling a long deep drag and letting the smoke filter through his nostrils, all the while staring down at the prisoner. Finally, Fowler spoke.

"I'd offer you a cigarette, but you don't deserve even that as far as I'm concerned. We can do this one of two ways; the easy way…or the hard way. I'm going to ask you two very simple questions. You can cooperate and answer quickly and peacefully. That would be the easy way. Then there's the other option. If you refuse to answer my questions, I'll beat you to within an inch of your life and leave you here to crawl around the floor in pain. I'm sure the precinct janitor would be happy to come in and mop up your blood. The last I saw of him, he looked pretty bored. Now…which option are we going to take, Piotr?"

The mobster looked up at Fowler. A know-it-all smirk came across his face.

"I wish to speak with an attorney now," Piotr said.

Fowler dropped his cigarette to the cell floor and stamped it out with the sole of his shoe. He came closer to Piotr. He slugged him in the jaw, sending him falling backwards as he sat, causing him to hit his head on the wall behind him with a dull thump!

"That would be the wrong option!" Fowler scolded him.

The gangster protested, blood trickling from the edge of his mouth.

"I know my rights! I want a lawyer!"

Fowler laughed. There was something cathartic about a bit of violence now and then, especially when it was aimed in a worthy direction. He was not about to put up with any of Piotr's nonsense.

"You might know your rights when you're dealing with the regular cops, you scum," said Fowler, "but you're locked in here with a federal agent now. The rules have changed! Now let's get back to my two simple questions. First, who do you work for? Second, where do I find him?"

Piotr rubbed his bruised jaw, but remained silent, simply staring at Fowler with growing scorn in his eyes. Fowler turned his back on Piotr for a moment.

"Turn around, Goldberg," the G-Man said through the bars. "You don't have to witness this."

The detective turned away and waited with his back to the cell. He did not see what was happening, but he heard it all. Fowler growled out his questions once more, but they were met with defiant silence. Then there was the thud of a fist hitting ribs, followed by a whimper of pain. Then the sound of another punch rang out, followed again by a whimper. The sound of a body slammed into a wall met Goldberg's ears, accompanied by a third cry of pain. He could hear the distinctive "plink" of a tooth hitting the hard floor. Finally, after many minutes of the music of violence and pain, Goldberg heard the gangster's accented voice, barely more than an anguished whisper, speak out.

"No more, no more, I beg you. I will speak."

Goldberg turned around, ready to resume watching the brutal spectacle. Piotr was sitting on the cell floor, leaning against the cot. His face was bloody and heavily bruised. He was clutching his abdomen, which had obviously had a close encounter with Fowler's fist. The G-Man was standing over him, lighting another cigarette.

"What is your boss's name?" said Fowler, for what felt like the thousandth time. "And where can I find him?"

Piotr was ready to tell Fowler everything he knew. "I do not know his real name. Nobody knows his real name. In his presence, we simply call him 'Sir.' You must understand that he rules over his men through the force of his will, his reputation as a master who shows no mercy, and sheer terror and fear. He is not entirely human! His face is hidden always from us, and it is believed by many that he only shows his true appearance to those who are about to die. I cannot tell you more about his identity, but perhaps I can give an answer to your second question. But I have a request. Please, Agent Fowler, send me to prison far away from this city…for his reach extends even into the jails…and even there I will not be safe from his vengeance!"

"We'll talk about that after I've seen how useful your information is," said Fowler. "Now tell me where he is!"

Piotr took in a deep breath, still in pain from Fowler's beating. "You were close to him already, Fowler. In the building where you came for your payment, he dwells in the penthouse on the highest floor, the tenth floor. Only I was allowed to visit him there; most of his business was conducted through me. He was near to us when you came to arrest me, and when you shot my bodyguards. He is doubtlessly already aware of what you have done…and that may mean that he has left that place. On the other hand, Agent Fowler, it may mean that he is still there, waiting for you, waiting for the moment when he will kill you!"

"Thanks," said Fowler, and he turned away. "Goldberg, let me out of here. Take care of our prisoner; I have things to do."

Goldberg unlocked the cell door, let Fowler out, and locked it again to keep Piotr in. "Fowler, I'm coming with you. You can't go after our mystery man alone. Who knows how many guards he has?"

"No, you're not coming with me," Fowler insisted. "Sometimes one man, alone, can be more effective than an army of cops. By myself, I can try to bypass the guards and the thugs and find a way directly to the man himself. If you don't hear from me in three hours, feel free to send in the cavalry."

Fowler grabbed his hat and jacket and walked out of the room.

It didn't take long for Fowler to make his way back to the building where he had arrested Piotr that morning. The police that had been there mopping up his mess had all departed by now. The corpses of the two thugs that he and Goldberg had shot were safely tucked away in the morgue. All police business was finished there, so Fowler could do what he had come to do. To use the front door would be stupid, he knew, since his visit might be expected. He decided to look for a rear entrance. He slinked down the alley along the side of the building. He moved with confidence and just enough speed to get where he needed to be quickly but without drawing unwanted attention to him. His gun was secured in his shoulder holster, but his right hand was always ready to reach for it at an instant's notice. He wished it were night, as the cover of shadows would make it easier to sneak about, but he could not wait for the daylight to leave Philadelphia; if his target had not already fled the area, he might do so soon. There was no time to waste.

Fowler reached the rear of the building without encountering anyone. He found a service door, marked with a sign designating it for use by employees only. Ignoring the signage, he tried the door and found it open. The door led to a narrow rear hallway with a door that led to a flight of stairs. Fowler looked up, happy to see that the steps seemed to lead all the way up to the topmost level of the structure, with a landing at each floor. He saw or heard no signs of anyone nearby. His instincts told him that it couldn't possibly be that easy, but his eyes and ears told him otherwise. He started up the stairs, optimistic but cautious. Walking quickly, but quietly, up ten flights of stairs was not what Fowler would have most liked to have been doing at that moment, but it was duty that called, so he kept going. Fowler was young and strong, so the strenuous climbing had little effect on him. Finally, he reached the top.

He paused in front of the door at the final landing at the highest level of the building. He drew his gun. He took a breath and shoved the door open. He walked into the room behind the door, eyes roving back and forth looking for any sign of danger.

The room was empty, much like the one where Fowler had arrested Piotr. This one did not even contain a single chair. All that was there was a man, alone, staring out the far window with his back to Fowler. The man was fairly tall, quite thin, dressed in what looked, from Fowler's place, to be normal clothing; black shoes, black pants, trench coat, and a derby. Fowler aimed his gun at the man's back.

"Don't try anything foolish," said Fowler. "If you're armed, toss your gun aside. Then I want you to raise your hands and turn around slowly. I won't hesitate to shoot if I see anything that alarms me."

"My dear Agent Fowler," the man replied, not turning around to face Fowler, "I am certainly armed, but it is not with a gun. You see, under this coat of mine, strapped around my ribs, are enough pieces of dynamite

"Thanks," said Fowler, and he turned away."

to blow the entire roof of this building to hell...taking you and I with it. So no, Agent Fowler, I am not going to turn around. And I would think twice before pulling that trigger. Even if your bullet kills me quickly, are you willing to wager that it will do so before my finger can squeeze the detonator trigger and cause the explosion that will end your life?"

Fowler kept his gun aimed at the suspect's back while he clenched his other hand in frustration. "How do I know you're not bluffing? Turn around and let me see the explosives."

"I will not," the man replied. "We are going to talk first. I am going to tell you who I am...or what I am. After that, provided you haven't given me a reason to detonate this dynamite, we will decide what we are going to do next. I could have found a way to kill you quickly and been done with all of this, but I chose not to. You see, Agent Fowler, I have never killed a federal agent before...and I wish to slowly savor the experience."

"Who the hell are you?" Fowler bellowed with noticeable annoyance. He was in no mood for games like this.

"My name is unimportant," was the reply. "You need not know who I am...as much as you will soon know what I am!"

Fowler decided to play along. In his experience, he had found that when a criminal enjoyed talking about himself, it could sometimes be an advantage to the agent facing the criminal. If one gets too caught up in conversation, he can lose his concentration on his surroundings.

"All right then," Fowler said. "If you want to tell me your life story, go right ahead. I'll admit that I'm curious as to how you just showed up here in Philadelphia recently, and have already managed to scare most of Smokey Wawelski's men into joining your little outfit...and killing those who wouldn't sign up! Why don't you turn around so I can see you as we talk?"

"No!" yelled the man, refusing Fowler's request. "I will allow you to see me when I am ready!"

"Fair enough," said Fowler, not wanting to aggravate his foe too much, fearing that such aggravation would lead to a deadly explosion.

"Fine," Piotr began to tell his tale. "You want to know why I killed Wawelski and took his place. I will tell you why! His place was my rightful place; his name was my rightful name! You see, Agent Fowler, I am his brother, his older brother, although he did not know that he had one! I was born in Poland; to the same parents as Stanislaw Wawelski, but several years earlier. In fact, those parents named me Stanislaw! His name should have belonged to me!

"There were, however, certain...complications that arose after my birth. I was born, as you shall see when I choose to let you see, terribly deformed. My mother, I was later told, was terrified to see the abomination to which she had given life! My father too, abhorred my appearance...and even went so far as to remark that I must have been the spawn of the devil! He decided to toss me away like a small bundle of rubbish, of trash! He took me from my mother's arms, not wanting his wife to ever have to set her eyes on my ugliness again. He planned to leave me out in the cold night where I would either freeze or starve to death…and probably be eaten by the wolves!

"There was, however, an ounce of mercy in that man's soul…and he could not bring himself to simply toss me among the rotting leaves of the ground. He rode to the encampment of a band of gypsies who were passing through the area, and he left me with them, knowing that my deformities would be a help, rather than a hindrance, to their way of life. People are often willing to pay to gawk at monstrosities…and I certainly fit into the category of potential exhibits. And so the gypsies raised me. I hold no ill will towards their kind, as they kept me warm and fed and sheltered for all of the earliest years of my existence. My first memories are of being among those people.

"I spent many years with my adopted family. We were a proud clan, living off of the money that the people willingly gave in order to witness strange spectacles and other entertainments. For my childhood, through my adolescent years, and on into my early adulthood, I was the lead attraction wherever my family of nomads chose to set up their tents and draw in the inhabitants of the nearest city or town.

"Unfortunately, I had been destined to be born at the end of the era of the wandering gypsies. As we moved into the twentieth century, progress interfered with the old ways. The coming of the motorcar, the radio, and the cinema took money from our hands as people found other ways to fill their leisure hours. The young ones among us drifted away, one by one, to find things to do among the more 'civilized' peoples of the world. Our traditions were dying and I knew that I had to find another way to survive. So, I ran off one night, determined to find another place in the world. I quickly learned to hide my appearance as much as possible. I learned the art of stealth, and I was able to travel throughout most of the European continent without being detected. I hopped onto freight trains, stowed away on boats. I eventually reached England, where I worked for a time as a member of what you might call a freak show. I hated it. It gave me some money with which to eat, but it lacked the warm, comfortable atmosphere of life among the gypsies of the more eastern sections of the continent. The one treasure I did gain there was the knowledge of your language, English. Once I had mastered that tongue, I chose to leave that part of the world and come to America.

"My adopted father, the patriarch of the gypsy clan had told me what he had known of my birth parents. I was able to find out what had become of them. I knew that my mother had died in Poland and my father and my younger brother, who had been given the name that had once been mine, had come to the United Stated. I vowed to make my first order of business to locate them and avenge myself for my abandonment!

"I found my father first…and he fell dead upon seeing my face! His old heart, worn from years of hard labor, could not stand the sight of my face in all its grotesque deformity. I was not sad to see him die.

"Next, I set out to find my brother, Stanislaw. I was astounded to see what he had made of himself; head of the most powerful gang of criminals in one of the nation's greatest cities! Then, in a sudden spell of inspiration, I understood my destiny! There are very few options in this world for a man of my unique traits. One is to be a sideshow attraction, making a living from the stares of a terrified but fascinated audience. I had had enough of that life! My other option, I realized, was much more enticing. I had been born with the face of a monster….and so I then chose to live the life of a monster! The rest, Agent Fowler, you already know. I killed Stanislaw, the man the city of Philadelphia knew as Smokey Wawelski, and I took his place, using fear, brutality, and intimidation to rise to be the new head of my little brother's empire of crime! And here, Agent Fowler, we stand; the law and the underworld, one of us about to die. Which will it be then, the man…or the monster?"

Fowler had listened intently to the entire speech. He had not been the least bit bored by it for, although he abhorred evil men such as this one, he also found them fascinating. It was his job to learn about evil, so that he could best decide how to combat it. Now, the long story had ended, and Fowler knew that violence had to come next. His fingers instinctively tightened around his gun. His shoulder and leg muscles tightened, preparing to act quickly and with certainty when his foe made a move.

The surviving Wawelski turned around, finally, and Fowler was able to see him from the front. His head, including his face, was completely concealed, covered by a hat and a thick scarf. Only two small holes were present, at the area of the eyes, allowing the mobster to see Fowler, but prohibiting the G-Man from seeing him. The rest of his body was covered as well, in his trench coat, with gloves upon his hands.

He took a step towards Fowler. The G-Man aimed the gun straight at him.

"Not another step," said Fowler. "Explosives or not, I'm not letting you come any closer."

Wawelski began to laugh. "You stupid, stupid man; have you never heard of the term 'bluffing?' I have no dynamite!"

He opened his coat, revealing a silk suit, but no sign of any weapons of any kind! Fowler was angry and shocked. He was stunned only for an instant, but it was long enough to give Wawelski the advantage. The criminal moved! It was with a speed that Fowler had never seen in a human being; with a leap propelled by powerful leg muscles, Wawelski slammed into Fowler, the two men falling to a heap on the penthouse floor! Fowler heard the "clunk" and "shoosh" of his gun falling from his grip, hitting the floor, and skidding away. He was now unarmed, and in a wrestling match with a madman!

Fowler knew what he had to do. During the longwinded speech that Wawelski had made him endure, Fowler had noted how many references had been made to the Polish crime lord hiding his appearance. When men were ashamed of their looks, Fowler knew, the most potent weapon against them could be a sudden unmasking. He reached up with one hand and tore the scarf from Wawelski's face.

Wawelski let out a strange, whooping cry, more animal in nature than human. He fell backwards off of Fowler and clasped his hands over his face, trying to conceal what Fowler had just exposed. Fowler started to stand. He could not see Wawelski's face, for his hands were large enough to cover it, but he could see that the mobster's hair was longer, thicker than it should have been and now spilled wildly down along the sides of his head.

Then, as quickly as he had put up his hands to block his face, Wawelski dropped them, letting the light that streamed in the penthouse's large windows illuminate his countenance. Fowler gasped at what he saw! Wawelski had, quite literally, the face of an ape! The leathery skin, the distorted nose with its large nostrils, the wild, animalistic eyes, and the jaggedly fanged mouth! Fowler was staring at a man with the head of a gorilla!

The ape-man pounced, hurling himself with tremendous force straight at the G-Man! Fowler felt his head hit the floor as he fell under the weight of the deformed criminal. It hurt, but Fowler remained conscious. Had he not, he would not have lived to see another sunrise, for the ape-man bared his fangs and moved his face with a sudden flurry of speed, teeth coming perilously near to Fowler's jugular! Fowler turned his head just enough to avoid the deadly bite!

The G-Man knew he was outmatched. Wawelski, although appearing thin, was pure animal muscle, stronger than Fowler, faster than Fowler, and filled with a berserker rage, pure murder on his mind. Fowler knew that only his own iron will and the merciless desperation that a man possesses when his life is at stake could save him from this beast of a man. He grabbed Wawelski's shoulders with both hands. He pushed upwards, muscles straining, forcing them both into a standing position. Then, Dan Fowler gave a mighty shove, pushing the ape-man away with all the strength he could find. He prayed that the glass that composed the windows of the penthouse was not too strong.

Wawelski flew backwards. He hit the window like a runaway train hitting a brick wall. The glass shattered! The ape-man fell!

Fowler walked over to the window, listening to the sound of the most inhuman scream he had ever heard. He looked down just as the body hit the pavement, exploding in a crimson mess that sent pedestrians into a horrified panic.

"Oh, Hell," the G-Man muttered to himself, envisioning the mountain of paperwork that would result from what he had just done.

"And so we give to the Earth the body of Carl Drummond. He was a patriot, guardian of the innocent, and dispenser of justice. He was a man who lived his life in service to his fellow man…and that is how his life ended. May he enter into eternal rest and find the peace that he fought for in his earthly life."

The minister finished his sermon. Slowly, the gathered colleagues, relatives, and friends of Detective Carl Drummond left the gravesite. Dan Fowler shook hands with Detective Goldberg, who thanked him for finding the men responsible for his partner's death. The two men parted company, and Fowler began to walk towards the cemetery's exit. As he walked, he saw a man leaning against the wall of one of the memorial park's mausoleums, smoking a pipe. The man's face was concealed by the shadows of both the wall and his fedora, but Fowler knew him immediately by his posture. The G-Man approached him.

"Hello, Chief," said Fowler.

The Chief extended his hand. "I don't thank agents. You're not children and you know your jobs. I give out assignments, you carry them out, we pay you, and then the cycle begins again. But…if I was ever going to thank an agent, this might be the time, Fowler. Carl Drummond was a true friend to me. You avenged him. I won't forget this, Fowler."

The Chief turned and walked away. Fowler took out a cigarette and lit it before resuming his walk.

Fowler made one more stop before the airport. He found himself sitting at a table in the *Declaration of Intoxication*, joined for a drink by a gorgeous brunette.

"So he's dead," said Marie. "Good. After what he did to Smokey, I'm glad to know you killed him. It's been a pleasure, Dan."

Fowler smiled at her. Although they were from opposite sides of the law, he found her to be charming, and more than a little attractive.

"What will you do now?" he asked her. "I hope you're not thinking of taking your adopted father's place and trying to lead the Philadelphia underworld. I have a feeling that might be more than a nice girl like you can handle."

Marie giggled. "The thought had occurred to me."

"Listen," continued Fowler, "I've seen the list of burglaries you're suspected of. Goldberg hasn't arrested you yet, out of respect for me and the help you gave us on this case, but once I've left this town behind you'll be fair game. Before I go, I have an offer to make."

Marie was intrigued. "It's not a marriage proposal is it?"

Fowler ignored what he hoped was a joke. He had no intention of settling down anytime soon.

"There's an old saying," he went on. "It takes a thief to catch a thief. I'll bet you know more about sneaking into places and stealing things than anyone else I've ever met. The people I work for could use some expertise like that. I have a feeling that a lot of your past sins might be forgiven…and eventually forgotten, if you'd give us a hand in that area. Why don't you settle your affairs here in Philly, and when you're ready you can fly down to Washington and we'll take it from there."

He handed her his card, with his direct number at the bureau offices. She took it, letting her slender fingers brush against his for one tantalizing moment.

"All right, Special Agent Fowler," she said with mock officiousness, "I'll see you soon."

The End

Dan Fowler: Monkey Business

"Influences"

I'm sitting here writing this essay to go with my second Dan Fowler: G-Man story and I realize that it's been over a year since I wrote "Monkey Business." That being the case, I had to go back and reread the thing to refresh my memory before starting this essay. I suppose I knew what favorite writers of mine were exerting an influence on me as I wrote it originally, but the rereading makes this even more apparent to me. I have a lot of favorite writers and if I were asked to name some of them, the list would likely change from day to day, but there are some who would make every list, especially if I was considering which writers had taught me things that I use when I write detective, crime or suspense stories, which are all categories into which this one falls. Two of those influential writers should be mentioned here and I'd like to dedicate this story to them. If I had the opportunity, I'd thank them both in person for the many hours of enjoyment their works have given me but, alas, one died over a decade before I was born and the other when I was just eight.

If ever there was one man who told great stories of crime on the big city streets, perpetrated by grotesquely disfigured criminal masterminds, that man was Chester Gould. From 1931 all the way into the 1970s when he retired and let various others take the reins, Gould's comic strip *Dick Tracy* graced the pages of almost all of America's newspapers and readers of all ages thrilled to the square-jawed police detective's war against such bizarre villains as Flat-Top, Pruneface, the Brow, and countless others. Tracy, unlike the more merciful heroes of the comic books, usually sent his foes to brutal deaths that poetically fit the nature of their crimes. The Brow, for example, was a Nazi agent who met the reaper by being impaled on a flagpole! I could never write a character like Dan Fowler without having some of Dick Tracy creep into the recipe. And we have a gangster who has the features of a monkey-man! That's pure Gould gold too. I'd probably never have thought that up without the memories of the excitement of reading those old Tracy stories when I was growing up.

As for the other writer I mentioned earlier, his name was Fleming. Ian Fleming. I've seen every James Bond movie probably half a dozen times, with the exception of the last one which, in my opinion, strayed so far from the formula that was so successful for so long that I couldn't stand to watch it again. When it comes to the very best of the Bond films, *Goldfinger, From Russia with Love, Dr. No,* and *On Her Majesty's Secret Service,* those are movies I could never get enough of. I've also read all of Fleming's Bond books, and if you haven't I'd recommend that you do so too; they're even better thrillers than any of the movies.

There's a reason that James Bond is one of the most influential, if not *the* most influential characters in heroic fiction of the second half of the twentieth century. That reason is that Fleming took everything a man often fantasizes about being and rolled them all up into one character. What male of the human species hasn't walked out of the movie theatre after seeing the latest Bond film, that great theme running through his head, and felt like he could conquer the world with smooth wit and quick thinking? After one of those movies, you can't help but walk out of the theatre a little more confidently, drive just a bit faster on the way home, and feel an overwhelming desire to sit at a casino sipping a martini and smooth talking the most gorgeous woman in the place into going up to your room with you. When Carly Simon sang the words "nobody does it better" as the opening song to one of the 70s Bond movies, she could just as well have been singing about Ian Fleming's ability to write great spy fiction. Whether I'm aware of it at the time or not, a bit of Bond sneaks into every heroic male character I write. There's a lot of him in my Hound-Dog Harker character, but he's in Dan Fowler too. Marie, the beautiful cat burglar could have been a Bond Girl too I think. There's even a line of dialogue in the story that also occurs at a very memorable moment in Fleming's Bond work. If you've read his books, you might recognize it. If you haven't, go out and get some.

Chester Gould and Ian Fleming were very different in many ways. Gould was an artist as well as a writer while Fleming's work was strictly literary. Fleming was British and Gould was American. Fleming's stories were international in scope and Gould's detective stayed in the states. Fleming's Bond is probably, and somewhat unfortunately, now better known in his film incarnation than as he is in the books, while Gould's Tracy is still most recognized exactly as Gould drew him rather than as he was portrayed by Warren Beatty in the 1990 film or by any of the actors in the movies of the Forties. But, despite the differences, it's one big similarity that really matters. Chester Gould and Ian Fleming both knew how to tell one hell of a good story. That's what counts.

AARON SMITH - is the author of numerous pulp stories for Airship 27 Productions, including stories in the SHERLOCK HOLMES CONSULTING DETECTIVE series, Black Bat stories, a Dan Fowler tale in the previous G-Man volume, and the Doctor Watson novel SEASON OF MADNESS. He is the creator of the pulp characters Hound-Dog Harker and the Red Veil. Other works include the science-fantasy novel GODS AND GALAXIES and stories for the Pro Se Productions line of magazines, as well as some work in comic books. Coming soon will be in a novella in QUATERMAIN – The New Adventures. Information about Smith's work can be found on his blog at www.godsandgalaxies.blogspot.com

in

"Proof of Supremacy"
by
Joshua Reynolds

It was 1938, and the echoes of gunfire had long since faded from the air. Spent bullet casings caught the sun as they rolled across the hard-scrabble street at the whim of a bone-dry breeze.

The First National Bank of Ogilvy, Illinois, had been hit in the early hours of the morning, its employees and early-bird patrons wiped from existence in a hurricane of lead and malice. Now, blood was smeared across the brand-new checkerboard tiles of the floor, and the vault door hung off of its hinges, charred and twisted.

A black Studebaker pulled up in front of the bank, and the local police on the scene shared a look that spoke volumes. The driver's door opened, and a long, lean shape unfolded and stepped out. The driver's eyes flicked down to the street, where they lingered on the bullet casings, then they swiveled back up, towards the crippled police car slumped in the street, bullet holes riddling the glass and wheels and front hood, then, finally, towards the burst open doors of the bank. Something big had hit them, at high speed.

"You can't park here," one of the officers on guard-duty spoke up, hitching his thumbs into his gun-belt.

"Hell I can't," Dan Fowler said, pulling his badge out of his coat pocket and flashing it. Fowler was six foot two and muscular, with dark hair and dark eyes that seemed to pierce whatever, or whoever, he was looking at. The cop flinched as Fowler's eyes scanned his face. "Inspector Fowler, FBI. Is everyone else inside?"

"Yeah," the other cop said, hiking a thumb over his shoulder. "They told us to expect you, so go on in."

"Obliged, gentlemen." Fowler stepped carefully through the doors, broken glass crunching beneath the soles of his wingtips. A guard lay near the door, half covered by a coroner's sheet, his shoes and twisted legs the only part of his body visible. Several other sheet covered shapes lay here and there, and Fowler restrained an instinctive growl.

There had been no need. Not for this. He shook his head. It was always the same…a car, usually stolen, sometimes rented, used to bust the doors off of their hinges. A burst of gunfire for any guards, then a second for any patrons, then, lastly, the tellers. The attacks were almost military in their precision.

Fowler had often been accused-or complimented, depending on the source-of having a mind like a filing cabinet. He stored facts and had the gift of easy recall. Unfortunately for him that recall included photos of similar scenes to this one…a parade of pitiful corpses, over twenty deaths, all attributable to one group.

Flashbulbs popped, and he grimaced as he was shaken out of his reverie. The vultures were already flocking. A knot of town fathers, featherers and fair-to-do's stood in the lobby, talking at one another as reporters, both the homegrown and out-of-town variety, circled them. Fowler's eyes zeroed in on the Police Chief-young for his title, but looking older by the minute. Ogilvy had only just incorporated earlier in the year, and this was likely the first time the newly-appointed Chief had been forced to even leave his office.

Fowler felt for him, but not enough to do more than nod in sympathy. Instead, he focused with laser-like precision on the too-familiar message scrawled across one wall of the bank, burned into the surface, even as it had been at every other bank he'd visited in the past six months:

And Put to Proof His High Supremacy...

Fowler took off his snap-brim hat and ran his hand over his slicked back hair, silently mouthing the four foot high words, as he had every other time he'd seen them. He'd read the book they'd come from cover to cover enough times to memorize it backwards and forwards.

"You know what it means?" someone said.

Fowler turned. "It's Milton. From *Paradise Lost*. Our boys are educated, if nothing else." He held out his hand to the Police Chief. "Dan Fowler, FBI. Chief Pasco?"

Pasco's eyebrows shot up. "You know me?"

"I like to get the lay of the land." Fowler shrugged. "Tom Pasco, the newly appointed police chief to the newly incorporated town of Ogilvy, in Crawford County, Illinois. You're one month into your term of service. And you've just had your first major crime."

Pasco's face was a picture of resignation. "And now you're here to pull my fat out of the fire, right?"

"Yes," Fowler said, bluntly. No sense beating around the bush.

"Was it the Mayor who called you?" Pasco said shooting a hot glare towards a man that Fowler assumed was the object of his ire.

"It was a mayor, sure," Fowler said. "Not yours, though."

"Small favors," Pasco said. He sighed and shook his head. "I'm up to my eyeballs in this, and I'm sinking quickly."

"You're the twelfth bank in twelve days that these gentlemen have hit." He turned and looked at the words. "And every time..."

"Think it's a message?"

"Yeah. Too bad I don't know what it means just yet," Fowler said. Pasco grunted.

"Thought you said it was from Milton?"

"It is." Fowler smiled slightly. "I just don't know who it's meant for yet."

"Is that important?"

"Quite possibly."

"When you figure it out, you'll let me know?" Pasco said.

Fowler nodded. "You and eleven other police chiefs. Not to mention mayors, senators, and congressmen." He gave a lazy salute. "No worries, Chief."

"So, what do you need from us?" Pasco said.

"Whatever you've got," Fowler said. "Every bit of information I collect goes towards putting together a picture of these guys."

Pasco nodded slowly. "They hit the place at ten on the dot, just after opening time. Rolled an old Ford right up through the doors like it was the most natural thing in the world. They had Thompsons, opened up on the place. Swept it clean," he said, hesitating slightly as his eyes flicked towards the nearest of the sheet-covered bodies. He licked his lips. "Blew the vault, probably with dynamite, maybe with nitro, then they beat feet."

"How long?" Fowler said.

"Five minutes. Maybe six." Pasco blew out a noisy breath and looked around, frowning. "It took us five minutes to get here. The car was already leaving the scene when we arrived."

"I saw the police car outside," Fowler said.

Pasco shrugged. "We tried to follow them. They let us know how they felt about that." He smiled weakly. "Almost cost us every police car the town owns. All two of them." He looked at Fowler. "Any of this sound familiar?"

"Unfortunately," Fowler said. He pulled a cigarette case out of his coat and flipped it open, offering it to Pasco. The Police Chief took one and stuffed it between his lips. He coughed as Fowler lit it.

"I don't smoke, but I'm thinking of taking it up after today," Pasco said, wheezing slightly. Fowler chuckled dryly and put one between his own lips.

"What about the getaway car?"

"Found it in a field about twenty minutes out of town. They'd set it on fire." Pasco scratched his cheek. "That's not news to you, is it?"

"No. It's not."

Pasco looked around, then back at Fowler. "What are you going to do now?"

"Have you collected any evidence from the scene?" Fowler said.

Pasco shook his head. "Didn't even know where to start, to be honest."

"Good thing I got here when I did, then." Fowler sucked in a lungful of smoke and expelled it through his nose. "I'll be back when the circus has left town," he continued, gesturing towards the reporters.

Pasco hitched up his gun-belt. "Want me to give 'em the boot?"

"No. Let them posture." Fowler scowled. "Best thing to do at times like this. Makes the citizens feel like everything is going according to plan." He watched the crowd, smoke curling gracefully out of the corners of his mouth. "Once they've had their fun, I can get to work."

Fowler waited out the press in the diner across the street from the bank. He worked on a plate of home fries and a cup of coffee with glacial slowness, letting his imagination play in the street.

He played the scene out again and again, backwards and forwards with movie reel clarity. All evidence to the contrary, he was lucky to get here when he did, he figured. Only a few hours behind, with a fresh scene to process.

He unrolled a map of the state, and glared at the red circles that denoted the banks that had been hit. All in Illinois, all in a very definite cluster, following the main county roads through Crawford and the surrounding counties. Close to 58,000 square miles of possible hiding places.

Twelve banks in twelve days. When did they sleep? When did they eat, or gas up the car? Even given how quickly you could move when you put your mind to it, it was still a feat of near impossibility.

He looked at the red circles again, measuring distance with his fingers and doing spatial calculations in his head. Every time, he came to the same conclusion-this wasn't one group, but several, all working in tandem.

Tandem implied organization, which implied the mob. Only Fowler knew that the mob guys didn't like working out of the city. And they weren't this precise.

He looked at his copy of *Paradise Lost*, sitting near his elbow. The book had been marked up six ways from Sunday as he tried to wring something-anything-from its pages.

Fowler leaned back in his seat, rubbing his brow with both hands, trying to grasp hold of the thoughts that teased the edges of his conscious mind. There was a piece missing. Something he wasn't seeing. With a sigh, he looked back at the map.

"A fan of Milton, I see."

Fowler's eyes popped open. Someone had taken the seat across from him, and that same someone was now bent over his map.

The guy was big, with the build of a swimmer, and a lithe insouciance to his posture. He had dark hair, a touch too long, and a hatchet face that beamed with good humor. "Milton," he said again, tapping the book with one long finger. "I never could get into it myself. I prefer Dumas for my light reading."

"Good to know. Why are you sitting at my table?"

"Not going to ask who I am?"

"Don't care about the who, just the why." Fowler fished his badge out of his pocket. "Inspector Fowler, Federal Bureau of Investigation."

"I thought G-Men usually came in pairs," the big man said, leaning back in his seat, arms extended across the length of the booth.

"I'm a special case."

"So I've heard." The big man smiled and stretched his hand towards Fowler. "Anthony. Jim Anthony. It's a pleasure to make your acquaintance, Inspector Fowler."

"Anthony as in the Waldorf-Anthony?" Fowler said, looking at the hand but not taking it. "As in the *Daily Star*? That Jim Anthony?"

"For my sins." Anthony inclined his head and pulled his hand back.

Fowler looked him up and down. "So you're the guy they call the Super-Detective, huh?" He knew how to size men up quickly, a useful skill for a government man to have. Anthony was a Person of Interest, and there was a file with his name on it in the Director's filing cabinet. A file that included numerous photos.

There were amateurs, and then there were Amateurs, and Anthony was of the latter variety. The Director wasn't a fan, but even he couldn't deny that Anthony had done some good. He dressed like a hobo longshoreman, with his baggy gray sweater and his linen trousers, but they said he moved like a leopard. Looking at him now, two feet away and as big as life, Fowler could believe them.

"Yellow journalism," Anthony said, shrugging. "Though, as monikers go, I've heard worse."

Fowler said nothing for a moment. If the silence disconcerted Anthony, the other man gave no sign. Finally, Fowler lit a cigarette and said, "So, investigating anything interesting, Super-Detective?"

"Call me Jim, please." Anthony waved away a curl of smoke and tapped the map. "And yes. A kidnapping, actually."

"A kidnapping, way out here in the sticks?"

"Saint Sebastian, actually. In the Caribbean."

Fowler grunted. "Taking the scenic route?"

"You found a woman's hat at the robbery in Perlmutter, the site of the first robbery," Anthony said, gesturing. "Cloche. Very high-end, with an expensive brooch on it. Not like anything that one of the three female victims there would have worn."

Fowler blinked. "How in the Devil did you know that?"

Anthony shrugged. "I have resources. I circulated images of the clothing my victim was wearing to various sources on the Federal and local levels nation-wide. *Et voila!*" He spread his hands. "The brooch on the hat was one of a kind."

"Yeah?" Fowler felt a stir of interest despite himself. "How one of a kind?"

"A shard from the Graybuck Stone."

Fowler whistled. The Graybuck stone had been one of the largest natural gemstones found on the North American continent, and had provided the foundation of the Graybuck fortune. Facts clicked into place.

"Graybuck. Harold Oliver Graybuck. Industrialist, right? Got a habit of donating obscene amounts of money to various charitable organizations?" Fowler said. He snapped his fingers. "The Annie Sanders case! Graybuck's ward. She got kidnapped two weeks ago, didn't she?"

"Got it in one, Agent Fowler. Graybuck is an—ah—associate of mine. He asked me to look into her kidnapping."

"I thought the Chicago Bureau office was handling the girl's case," Fowler said.

"Say woman, rather. Sanders turned eighteen two weeks ago," Anthony said off-handedly. "But yes, they are. And, unfortunately, they're short-handed."

"So you're just doing your civic duty, huh?"

"It's nice to give back," Anthony said.

"So why are you here, crowding me, and not heading to-where'd you say?"

"Saint Sebastian. Because of the hat, mainly. And because the evidence the Chicago offices had at their disposal was sorely lacking." Anthony shook his head. "It was all circumstantial. Nothing concrete."

"But the hat is as concrete as it gets?" Fowler said.

"That shard of stone says I'm on the right track," Anthony said.

"Say I agree," Fowler said, leaning back. "What does the one have to do with the other?"

"I have no idea." Anthony turned his attention to the map. "But I was heading to the site of the last robbery when I heard about this one. I thought a fresh scene might prove beneficial to my investigation."

"And you came to ask my permission?" Fowler said, smiling slightly. "Neighborly of you."

"I like to work with duly appointed representatives of the law enforcement community when I can." Anthony looked up from the map. "Besides, two heads are better than one."

Fowler puffed quietly on his cigarette, considering. He wished that he'd had the time to roust Kendal, or one of the others, to come with him. Extra hands made swifter work, and he had a feeling that this case was going to require backup before it was over. He looked at Anthony, and came to a decision.

"Fine. This is my case, though."

"Of course."

"I get the credit," Fowler said.

"I wouldn't have it any other way." Anthony extended his hand again. "Shake on it?" Fowler took his hand, and then stubbed out his cigarette.

"Scene's clear," he said, gesturing out the window. The sun was dipping past the horizon, and the sky was the color of ripe plums as the media vultures scattered to the four winds. Fowler finished his last fry and drained the dregs of his coffee and he and Anthony stepped out of the diner and strode across the street. Fowler, calculating bullet trajectories in his head, said, "What do you know about these robberies so far?"

"A car crashes through the doors at opening time, or a little after. Three quick bursts of gunfire. Then they vanish. How many perpetrators were involved, would you say?"

"Five, judging by witness statements and the angle of the shots," Fowler said absently as he retrieved a flashlight from his car and headed up the stairs. The bank had been emptied, the bodies removed, but it still stank of blood and gunpowder.

"No matter how many times I see scenes like this, it never gets any easier," Anthony murmured.

"When it does, it's time to quit," Fowler said as he held out a hand and moved around the chalk outlines, measuring the height and the angle of the shots with the beam from the flashlight. The car hadn't stopped moving until it hit the velvet rope that marked the third teller window. The rope stand was bent where the car had come into contact with it.

"Well, the Milton makes sense now," Anthony said, looking up at the wall. "*Paradise Lost.*"

"Bingo," Fowler said. "At every scene, the same phrase."

"Interesting. Look at this," Anthony said as he dropped to his haunches and brushed his fingers across the tire tracks. Fowler copied him. Lifting his hand, he rubbed his fingers together, feeling the loose soil that coated them.

"Cigarette butts," Anthony said.

"Maybe the customers smoked."

"Maybe they didn't," Anthony said, holding up a cigarette butt. "Cigarettes are a wealth of information, if you look closely enough."

Fowler ignored him, concentrating on the tire tracks. Dark mud. Traces of something else. Only, the streets outside were newly paved. Fowler frowned. A staging area, then?

Probably just outside of town, in that case. Since the oil boom, there were plenty of abandoned farms and homesteads in the surrounding area, sold off to out-of-town speculators. He'd familiarized himself with the immediate area before he'd arrived, working out a mental map to navigate by. He knew of four possible locations within easy driving distance.

"Smell that?" Anthony said, still crouched over the tire tracks. Almost delicately, he sniffed his fingers.

"Smell what?"

"Manure. The flowery bouquet of the farm," Anthony said. "Wherever they set out from, there were cows there."

Four locations shrunk to one possibility in Fowler's mind. "There's a dairy farm just outside of town. Owned by a family named Mueler according to the county records."

"You read the county records?" Anthony said.

"Only the pertinent ones," Fowler said, already swooping towards the doors and the black Studebaker still parked outside. Anthony hurried after him.

"Are we going to inform the local authorities?"

"No time. Get in," Fowler snapped. Anthony climbed in even as Fowler pulled away from the curb with a screech of rubber.

"I guess you already know how to get there, then?" Anthony said, clutching at his seat as Fowler took a sharp turn.

Fowler tapped the side of his head. "Best road atlas in the Bureau. You packing?"

"No. I left my pistol in my car."

"There's an old saying, 'never stray more than arm's length from your gun,'" Fowler said.

"I prefer 'never get into a situation where a gun is necessary,'" Anthony said. "I can take care of myself."

"You're going to have to. We're not going back for it."

"You believe they're still in the area?"

"I think we can't take the chance they aren't." Fowler spun the wheel, slapping it around as if it'd insulted him.

"How many people live at the farm?" Anthony said.

"Two according to the records," Pasco said. "A man and a woman." Then, "Frank and Abigail Mueler." The map unfolded in his head as he hit the town limits. The Mueler place was three miles out of town. It was a registered dairy farm, which meant inspections, which meant the government knew where it was. And if the government knew, so did Fowler.

He caught the farmhouse in his headlights twenty minutes later. It sat at the end of a stubby country road, still muddy from the previous evening's rain. A lopsided barn sat nearby, the doors swinging open in the night breeze. One crashed back against the wall with a loud rattle over and over again.

Fowler hit the brakes as an untended cow wandered in front of the Studebaker. "Think that's normal?"

"No. They should be locked up for the night," Anthony said, stepping out of the car, fists clenched. "Damn."

"Go slow, Super-Detective," Fowler said.

Anthony glanced at him. "I'll take the barn, G-Man. You take the house." Then, with surprising swiftness, he loped towards the barn, body held low. Fowler watched him for a moment, and then headed for a house.

Pistol held close, he bent his knees and darted forward, hoping to avoid notice if anyone was inside looking out.

Shoulder braced against the frame of the front door, he tried the knob. The door swung open. Fowler silently counted to three, and swung himself inside, the automatic rising. He swept the room and then moved onto the next. The kitchen.

Fowler pressed his knuckles to the stove, and found it still warm. There was wood inside, and the red glimmer of active embers just below it. He turned, taking in the rest of the kitchen. Food on the table, butter melting in the dish. Someone had eaten dinner here, recently.

Upstairs, a floorboard creaked. Fowler's head went up, and his eyes narrowed. Could be nothing, or could be something. There was still no sign of the Muelers, which didn't bode well.

He started for the stairs, but then whirled as a pistol bellowed from the direction of the barn. Cursing, Fowler hit the door at a run. He slowed as he neared the barn.

"Anthony?" he called.

No reply.

Fowler kicked aside the barn door and stepped into the darkness. There was a battered truck parked in the center of the barn. From above him, several strands of hay drifted down. He froze, and looked up.

Something black lunged for him from the hayloft. A jarring blow slapped aside the Colt, sending it spinning from his grip. Fowler stumbled back, raising an arm to block a second, rapid blow. His foot looped out instinctively, catching his opponent's ankle. A fist caught him in the side as the shape fell. Fowler slid aside and fell into a crouch as the shape bounced to its feet.

The shadowy shape came for him again with feline quickness, and fingers like iron hooks dug into his wrists as he was driven back into the wall, dislodging a number of tools. Eyes like twin suns blazed into his own and Fowler felt the strength suddenly bleed from his limbs.

It was an odd sensation, at once like drowning and smothering. Ignoring the feeling, he twisted, hauling his opponent around and hurling him to the floor. Unfortunately, whoever he was, he didn't release his grip, and Dan found himself jerked off his feet and slung bodily into the side of the truck.

A fist lashed out, and he slid down as it connected with the truck, denting the metal and eliciting a frustrated grunt from his attacker. Fowler took the opportunity to bulldog forward, driving his shoulder into his opponent's midsection, and sending them both careening out of the barn and into the night.

Bones aching, Fowler hauled himself to his feet and began to rifle through his coat. "All right pal," he grunted, flashing his badge. "Dan Fowler. FBI. Just in case you weren't sure if you were in trouble before."

The badge was kicked out of his grip, and he wobbled, hand gone numb.

"Fowler, move!"

Fowler threw himself to the side as Anthony crashed into the shape. They fell in a tangle, trading blows. Then they broke apart, as Anthony was shoved back against the front of the truck, something long and flat in his hands.

But before Fowler could move in pursuit of the other man, a rifle spoke once, sharply. The dirt at Fowler's feet was kicked up in a gout that spattered against his face.

Anthony tackled Fowler as a second shot followed on the heels of the first, plucking at the dirt again. They scrambled behind the dented vehicle.

"Go slow, Super-Detective."

"Hell." Fowler looked at Anthony. "Ambush?"

"I think we interrupted a getaway, actually," Anthony said, peering around the end of the truck. "Sounded like a carbine. Military issue." He looked at Fowler, who nodded. "Speaking of which, here's the gun our friend in the barn tried to perforate my skull with." Anthony passed Fowler a gleaming colt.

Fowler checked the pistol. "Think you can draw their fire, Super-Detective?"

"Don't kill them, if you can help it," Anthony said, frowning.

"Squeamish?"

"I'd like to question them, actually. Super-Detective, remember?" Anthony said, before shooting to his feet and vaulting over the roof of the truck. Fowler blinked in shock, and then stood, taking aim at the darkened window as a patter of rifle shots split the night.

Anthony moved through the rain of lead like a fish through water, almost swimming past the bullets. Fowler's automatic chewed up the windowsill, forcing the unseen shooter away from the window. Anthony leapt up, grabbing the edge of the roof long enough to swing himself up.

Fowler held his fire as Anthony barreled towards the open window and dove through. One last rifle shot sounded, then silence. Fowler raced towards the door, and inside.

"Anthony?" he called out, hesitating a half-second before he started up the stairs.

"I'm fine. You?" Anthony said as he appeared at the top of the stairs.

"You got him?"

"Of course-"

The growl of an engine interrupted Anthony and both men turned as a car speared past the front door. It struck Fowler's Studebaker with a shuddering crash, and then peeled off, heading away.

Fowler rushed out, firing his automatic at the departing vehicle, but to no avail. Upstairs, he found Anthony hog-tying an unconscious man with ripped up bed sheets.

"They got away."

"Not all of them," Anthony said, indicating the man on the bed. The man was dressed in a utilitarian outfit, a boiler suit, maybe, by the look of it, and a metal mask. The mask was featureless, save for a wide slit for the eyes, and air holes punctured into the lower half. He was breathing heavily as Anthony jerked him to his feet and tossed him onto the bed.

Fowler looked around the room, his eyes drawn instantly to the dark stains on the floor. He looked up at Anthony, who nodded.

"In the bathroom," he said quietly. Fowler glanced at the door to the room in question, and sniffed. Anthony made a face. "Wood chips and lye. For the smell."

"How long?" Fowler said, staring at the bound man.

"A few days. Maybe longer. Without an autopsy, I can't be sure."

"It doesn't matter," Fowler said, leaning over the man. With quick fingers he pulled off the mask and flung it to Anthony. Then, equally swiftly, he grabbed the man's jaw in a painful grip.

The man was young, but no kid. A few years younger than either Fowler or Anthony. His eyes popped open in shock and pain as Fowler jerked his head forward.

"Who are you?" Fowler said.

The man said nothing, his eyes flickering back and forth between Fowler and Anthony. Fowler shook him the way a terrier might shake a rat. "Answer me, kid. Why'd you try and pop us?"

Silence. And not a stubborn silence either. The young man's eyes were opaque, as if he were high to the gills.

"Tough guy, right? I get it." Fowler glanced at Anthony. "Give me some alone time with this fine young gentleman."

"Or, I could persuade him to talk without possibly killing him in the process," Anthony said, tossing the mask to Fowler, who leaned back, catching it awkwardly. "Handmade, by the way."

"What? The mask?" Fowler turned it over in his hands.

"Yes. In a workshop, probably." Anthony lifted up his sweater to reveal something that looked to Fowler like a money-belt. But instead of a wad of bills, Anthony popped open one of the pouches and pulled out what looked like a yellowish pill. He saw Fowler watching him and bounced the pill on his palm. "Relax. It's an amobarbital derivative I designed. Perfectly safe."

"Truth serum?" Fowler said, frowning.

"You know it?" Anthony's eyebrows rose. "I'm impressed, Inspector Fowler."

"Just because I've got a badge doesn't mean I also don't occasionally read a book, Anthony."

"I didn't mean to imply-"

"Save it." Fowler picked up the fallen rifle and sat down on the window sill. With practiced movements he ejected the spent brass and caught it on the fly. "You were right. Military issue. Even the ammo." He closed his eyes, thinking. "A truck went missing around two months ago. Heading for Camp Swampy."

"The papers said that was a laundry truck," Anthony said.

"You believe everything you read in the papers?"

"In my paper? Yes," Anthony said. He had the gunman's jaw in one hand and was using the other to massage his throat. "You're implying that it was a truck full of rifles?"

"And ammunition. And a few other things," Fowler said. "But that was

God knows how many miles away!" He set the rifle down with a thump. "How long is this stuff going to take to work?"

"A few minutes. It needs to be fully absorbed into his bloodstream," Anthony said.

Fowler grunted and rose to his feet. "Fine. I'm going to see if I can raise the locals. Let them know what happened. If he starts talking…"

"I'll yell," Anthony said.

"See that you do," Fowler said, heading for the stairs. Outside, he found that the Studebaker had expired. There were thin plumes of steam escaping through several bullet holes in the hood, and one of the wheels had been popped by the impact with the other car. Fowler shook his head and moved to see if the radio still worked.

As he tried to raise the local police-band, he caught sight of the thing Anthony had pulled off of their second attacker. It was a thick fold of material, dark blue in color. Roughly three meters in length, it had a thread tracks down the center.

It struck a chord, but Fowler couldn't recall where he'd seen such a thing before. He draped it over his shoulder and concentrated on rousting Pasco's department.

Twenty minutes later, the town's one working police cruiser, carrying the Mayor and the Chief of Police came bumping and jolting down the dirt road, followed closely by a hearse.

He fielded a scattergun burst of questions, not all of them hostile, and went back upstairs as they loaded the Muelers' bodies into the hearse. Anthony met him at the bedroom door. "He's ready to talk," he said.

"Anything interesting to say?"

"Ask him yourself," Anthony said. "You can have first crack at him."

Fowler grinned mirthlessly. He sank to his haunches in front of the gunman, who sat on the edge of the bed, eyes slightly glazed and his face slack.

"Who are you?"

"Paul Brackett," the gunman said.

"Why were you waiting here?"

"Supposed to burn the house. Get rid of the evidence."

"Why'd you shoot at us?" Fowler said.

"No witnesses," Brackett said.

"That answers my next question." Fowler glanced at Anthony. "Hand me that mask." Anthony did so and Fowler took it, holding it up in front of Brackett. "Why the fancy mask, Paul?"

"Brotherhood," Paul muttered.

Fowler's eyes narrowed. "What kind of brotherhood?"

"Brothers in arms."

"Who are they?" Fowler said.

"Dead men," Paul said.

"Who was your pal? The guy who got away?"

"The Master."

Fowler growled and looked back at Anthony. "I need a straight answer here."

"And you should be getting one," Anthony said, arms crossed, head bowed in thought. "He's not resisting, not actively. It's almost as if there's a-"

Brackett shuddered suddenly, writhing like an animal in a trap. As both Fowler and Anthony lunged for him, blood gushed from the gunman's mouth in a red torrent and he pitched backwards with a hideous gurgle.

"What in the name of God," Fowler breathed, hauling Brackett up by the front of his uniform. "He's dead."

Anthony used two long fingers to pry Brackett's mouth open with a sickening crackle-pop. He gagged and turned away. "His tongue. He chewed through it."

"Why the Hell would he do that?"

"He shouldn't have been able to! Not in the state he was in!" Anthony barked, running his hands through his hair. "Damn it!"

Fowler let the body flop back onto the bed and his hands clenched into fists. "What the hell is going on here? Bank robbers don't just off themselves, not in my experience."

"Nor in mine," Anthony said. He peered at the body. "Post-hypnotic suggestion?"

"What?"

"Nothing," Anthony said, gesturing sharply. "I emptied his pockets."

"Anything interesting?"

"Just this," Anthony said, holding up a scrap of paper that turned out to be a section of a map. There was a red circle around a name. "Denville."

"What's a Denville?"

"A town."

"With a bank? A new bank?" Fowler said.

"Almost certainly." Anthony shook himself and looked at Fowler. "I think it's the next target."

"I think you're right." Fowler looked back at the body on the bed. "You moved pretty quick back there."

"Best way not to get shot."

"Good point. What do you make of this?" Fowler said, suddenly recalling the length of material over his shoulder. "You pulled it off our long-gone friend."

Anthony took the material and examined it for a moment. While he looked at it, Fowler picked up the mask Brackett had been wearing.

"This is a *dastar*. A double *patti*, to be exact," Anthony said. "A turban."

"Hunh." Fowler scrubbed his thumb across the mask, trying to remove a layer of dirt.

"What do you see?" Anthony said.

"Random numeral placement," Fowler said, tapping a shallow scratch just above the eye-slits of the mask. "Roman numerals, to be exact."

"Thirteen," Anthony said, eyes narrowing. "Ring any bells?"

"Not offhand."

"Twelve banks so far." Anthony looked back at the body. "Symbolism? Or maybe they number each other to keep track…"

"Unlucky thirteen," Fowler said softly. He looked at Anthony and plucked the scrap of paper out of his hand. "I've got a map in the car." He paused. "The car itself is shot, though. Literally."

"I think I can do something about that," Anthony said, smiling crookedly.

They caught a ride back to town in the police car. Fowler stretched the fabric of the turban between his hands as they rode. "Who'd be wearing a turban in rural Illinois?"

"The United States has a substantial Asian population," Anthony said, examining the interior of the mask. "This mask was definitely a last minute job. Hastily soldered, badly patched."

"Which means?"

"I don't know."

"Thanks. You're a big help."

Brackett's body had been left where it lay, until the hearse could be pressed into service to return to pick it up. As Anthony went to get his car, Fowler talked to Pasco, keeping him in the loop as he'd promised.

"Call the Chicago Bureau offices. Get someone out here to take possession of that body," Fowler said, offering Pasco a cigarette. The Chief declined with a shake of his head.

"Happy to do it. No churchyard around here will take him, considering what he did to the Muelers." He pushed the brim of his hat up and said, "Was that really Jim Anthony?"

"Yes," Fowler said. "Why?"

"Think you can get me his autograph? Only see I'm a fan of those Spicy Detective stories, and they're supposed to be based on his-"

"I'll look into it," Fowler said, tersely.

Before Pasco could reply, a gleaming white Rolls-Royce skidded around the corner and shot towards them, causing Pasco to hop back with a yelp. It braked with the grumble of a powerful engine, and Anthony half-stepped out, leaning across the open driver's side door.

"Ready to go?" he said.

"You believe in traveling in style, don't you?" Fowler said as he got in.

"More about comfort, with me." Anthony gunned the engine and pulled out into the street, scattering a gathered flock of reporters in the process.

Fowler had his map unfolded across his half of the windshield as Anthony drove. "Denville," Fowler said, stabbing a finger into the map.

"How far is it?"

"Depends on how fast you drive."

The Rolls gave a deep growl as Anthony pressed the gas pedal down. "The engine runs on my own special blend of fuel. Hard to synthesize, but the benefits are worth it," Anthony said.

Fowler grunted. "We'll see." Frowning, he bent over the map, tracing his fingers across it. "It's got to be more than one group."

"Or a large group, divided into smaller squads," Anthony said. "A standard military practice. Flying squads, they're sometimes called."

"I know what they're called," Fowler said. "What I want to know is why these particular banks?"

"Targets of opportunity?"

"Does that feel right to you?" Fowler said.

"No. Maybe if the Sanders kidnapping wasn't tied in," Anthony said.

"Which we still don't know for sure."

"Don't we?" Anthony said. There was an obvious pause, and Fowler felt his attention sharpen. He looked at Anthony, squinting.

"What is it?"

"What's what?"

"What do you know, Anthony?"

"I told you to call me Jim, Inspector," Anthony said.

"And I'll be calling you booked for obstruction of justice if you don't talk." Fowler began to fold up the map. "Are we working together, or are we not?"

Anthony sighed. "Fine. Graybuck."

"And?"

"The twelve banks that have been hit so far? They're his." Anthony looked at Fowler. "When he asked me to investigate, I did some digging. His money was used to fund the banks, though he did it under the auspices of several shell corporations. I assumed he was being charitable."

"Well, if there's one thing you tycoon-types are known for, it's generosity."

"I donate almost half of my annual earnings to various charitable foundations and philanthropic organizations. I also spend a good deal of my free time solving crimes."

"For rich friends and acquaintances."

Anthony's jaw clenched. Fowler shook his head. "I'm not knocking you, Anthony. Don't get me wrong. Justice is justice, and anyone who pursues it with your kind of vigor is okay in my books, but I've come to learn a few things in my line."

"About the benevolence of tycoons?"

"That social class is often no guarantee of behavior." Fowler blew out a breath. "Something I bet you know."

"Yes," Anthony said, after a moment. "Do you know why I do what I do, Inspector?"

"A sense of civic duty?" Fowler said, only half-joking.

"I like to hunt," Anthony said.

"Deer?"

"Men." Anthony looked at him, his face calm and mask-like. "The thrill of it. The adrenaline that this kind of thing provides."

"I never pegged you for a thrill-seeker," Fowler said.

"Another guilty secret," Anthony said. "I have a lot of them."

"Most of us do, to one extent or another." Fowler leaned back in his seat. "If I quoted Machiavelli, would it help?"

"Interestingly, that's actually a contextual misquote," Anthony began, but stopped when he caught Fowler's look. He smiled. "I take your point, though."

"Good. Now that that's out of the way, get back to Graybuck."

Anthony nodded. "When the Crawford County oil-boom hit, Harry decided to turn Illinois into his pet project."

"Harry?" Fowler said.

"You can call me Jimmy, if it makes you feel better," Anthony said, smiling slightly.

"Illinois," Fowler prompted.

"He's been funding a number of small-town urban invigoration efforts. Giving something back, he calls it," Anthony said.

"By building banks."

"Among other things," Anthony said. "Regardless, he's pumping money into a number of small towns."

"How many, off-hand?" Fowler said.

"Thirteen," Anthony said quietly. "That's why I suspect that our band of merry robbers are targeting Graybuck's banks specifically."

Fowler snarled and struck his temple with the heel of his palm. "For the love of-how could I have been so stupid?"

"What?"

"The money!" Fowler snapped. "You said Graybuck was behind those banks, right? What if this ain't just about the banks themselves, so much as it's about who put what where?"

Anthony's eyes widened slightly. "The money-"

"Bingo." Fowler snapped his fingers. "We see it all the time at the Bureau. Some rich wiseacre will open a company, or a service or something and funnel money into it, to hide it. Hell, sometimes they even make donations to their own charitable causes."

"I never pegged Harry for the type." Anthony frowned.

"Regardless, maybe we need to pay a visit to Mr. Graybuck."

"Maybe so." Anthony frowned. "Denville first."

"Denville first."

The Rolls roared on, charging through the night and at last into the orange light of dawn several hours later. Fowler awoke with a start, having slipped into a cat-nap at some point. He pulled his hat off of his face and looked around.

"Denville?" he said.

"Such as it is," Anthony said.

Fowler grinned mirthlessly at the big-city prejudice in Anthony's voice. He sat up. At first glance, Denville was a carbon-copy of Ogilvy. The same small-town streets and store-fronts. America in miniature, Fowler had heard someone call such places, once.

He glanced at Anthony, seeing no signs of strain or exhaustion, despite the other man having driven through the night. Fowler himself felt like ten miles of bad road, despite the nap. He wondered how Anthony did it, and then wondered whether he had any choice. Fowler was a career-man, a crime-buster by inclination and profession. Anthony was a hunter by blood.

"Any sign?" Fowler said.

"No." Anthony blinked. "Wait…hear that?"

"No?" Fowler looked around. Anthony hit the brakes as an explosion rocked the street ahead of them. Fowler ducked his head as chunks of wood and stone crashed against the Rolls' windshield. He looked up. "Yes. Yes, I definitely heard that."

"Hang on," Anthony said, tapping the gas and letting the Rolls shoot forward. Fowler pulled his pistol and had his door open a moment later.

As before, a car had been used to batter aside the doors of the bank. The smoke rolling out through the wrecked entryway attested to the destruction of the vault. Any minute now, the getaway car would be backing out.

As Anthony pulled the Rolls in front of the doors, Fowler moved around the front, his automatic clutched in both hands. Pressing his shoulder to the doorframe, he swung around, raising his weapon.

"Federal agent! Freeze!" he snarled into the dispersing smoke.

A Thompson roared out a Chicago hymn in reply. Fowler ducked back against the wall. Anthony loped to join him, pistol in hand.

"Safe to say that they're in there."

"Really Sherlock? How'd you deduce that?" Fowler said. "Any thoughts on how to go about this?"

"Quickly?"

"It's going to get bloody," Fowler said.

Anthony's face went as stiff as stone. Then he tossed his pistol to Fowler. "Keep them bottled up."

"What are you going to do?"

"I'm going to go hunting," Anthony said, rummaging in his belt again. He pulled two small gel spheres out, one red and one blue, and pressed his palms together. There was a sound like glass crunching then a thin whisper of smoke slid through the spaces between Anthony's fingers. Then, before Fowler could stop him, he darted into the bank, flinging his hands out.

Moments later, thick clouds of colorful smoke burst into existence, mingling with the black memory of the vault explosion. Fowler grinned and shook his head. He'd seen a number of Anthony's tricks in the past few hours, and read about others, but seeing them in action never failed to amuse him.

Then came the screams and gunfire and Fowler's grin slipped. He heard the growl of an engine and a battered Ford backed out of the bank. Fowler leapt forward, climbing up onto the running board even as the car crashed into Anthony's Rolls.

"I said 'freeze' and I damn well meant it," Fowler said, aiming one of the automatics at the driver. The latter was clad in much the same way as Brackett had been, right down to the metal mask. The man jerked around, eyes widening.

"Holy-"

"Not quite, but thanks for the compliment," Fowler said. "Put the brake on. Now!"

Before the driver could comply, a Thompson, perhaps the same one from before, spat out a hail of lead as its wielder stalked out of the smoke. The front of the Ford was chewed up, and the driver jerked back and forth. Fowler shoved himself backwards, firing as he hit the street. The gunman staggered, his next flurry of shots going wild. Fowler fired again and he pitched backwards.

A carbine barked and Fowler rolled aside as a bullet tugged at his sleeve, losing his hold on one of the automatics in the process. Two more men stepped out of the bank, one leaning on the other. The rifleman tossed aside his weapon and clawed at the revolver stuffed through his belt. The other stumbled towards the Ford, jerking the driver's body out and climbing in.

"Come on!" he called out. The other man didn't reply, instead taking careful aim at Fowler.

"Drop the gun, pal," Fowler said, his arm extended awkwardly due to his prone position, but the barrel of his remaining pistol never wavering.

"Drop yours, 'pal'," the gunman replied.

"Get in the car!" the one behind the wheel shouted.

"Drop the gat, get on your knees, hands behind your head," Fowler grated. "I won't ask a third time."

"No. You won't." The hammer of the revolver made a loud sound as it was cocked. Fowler pulled his trigger a second later, but the automatic only made a dull 'click'.

Before his opponent could fire, however, Anthony lunged out of the smoke, fingers spread like the talons of some great bird of prey. He crashed into the gunman, driving him into the front of the Ford, then spinning him around and smashing a fist into his gut hard enough to pick him up off of his feet. The revolver went off, plucking a wedge out of the pavement as the gunman folded up around Anthony's fist.

The Ford was thrown into gear and it shoved the Rolls aside with a scream of tortured metal and breaking glass, then it shot off, heading out of town.

Anthony helped Fowler to his feet. "We've got to go after them!" Fowler said, starting towards the Rolls.

"No need," Anthony said, gesturing. Seconds later, a trio of police cars roared past the bank, sirens blaring. A fourth screeched to a halt.

Fowler held up his badge as the officers got out, service revolvers aimed at the two men. "Federal agent, boys."

"Press," Anthony said, holding up a press pass.

"Press?" Fowler muttered.

"I own a paper. That makes me Press. Technically."

"Technically," Fowler said. "Thanks, by the by."

"Think nothing of it," Anthony said amiably.

"What the hell happened here?" one of the cops said, as they lowered their pistols.

"We were having a party. What's it look like?" Fowler said. "You guys got here quick."

"Mr. Anthony radioed ahead," one of the officers said. "We thought it was a prank call, at first. Then we heard the explosion-"

"Yeah. Bet it didn't seem so funny then." Fowler turned, looking at the man Anthony had knocked out. "He going to kill himself too?"

"We'll see what we can do to prevent it," Anthony said. "There's another one inside."

"Alive?"

"I wouldn't have mentioned it otherwise," Anthony said. "I managed to interrupt them before they got to the customers."

Fowler grunted and stalked into the bank, waving his arms in an attempt to disperse the lingering smoke. The gunman lay on the polished floor, facedown and limp. Fowler hooked his foot under the man and rolled him over.

He glanced over at the bank patrons as the police questioned them. Scared and shaken, but alive. As far as he was concerned, that put them ahead of the game.

Fowler dropped down and removed the gunman's mask. Another boy next door. A little older, maybe.

"That's Tom Hitch!" someone said.

Fowler glanced around. One of the local cops was standing behind him, eyes wide. "You know this guy?" he said.

"Tom Hitch. He was from around here, but-"

"...he darted into the bank, flinging his hands out."

"But what?"

"He's supposed to be dead!"

"Hunh." Fowler frowned and stood. "Come here," he said, grabbing the officer's shoulder and maneuvering him to the door. "What about this guy?" He gestured to Anthony as they exited. "Get his mask off."

"What is it?" Anthony said, obliging.

"Phil Blum," the officer said, as the mask came off. He looked at Fowler. "What's going on here? He's supposed to be dead too!"

"Dead?" Anthony said, quirking an eyebrow.

"Dead. Didn't that Brackett kid mention something about dead men?"

"Brackett? Paul Brackett?" the officer said, looking from one man to the other.

"You know him too?" Fowler said, incredulously.

"I know them all! We got a damn monument to them in the center of town!" the officer blurted. "There's a photo and everything. Hitch's momma put it up!"

"Monument?" Fowler said, looking at Anthony.

Five minutes later, with the two gunmen unconscious and restrained, and the police in charge of the scene, Fowler and Anthony found themselves looking up at a granite slab, with a plaque mounted on it.

"The Crawford Oil-Rig Explosion of 1936," Anthony said. "Of course."

"Of course?" Fowler snorted. "Is this a clue, Shamus?"

"Thirteen men died in the explosion." Anthony tapped the plaque. "Or not, as it turns out."

Fowler took off his hat and ran a hand over his head. "I hate mysteries. Have I mentioned that?" He slapped his hat back on his head. "Great. So we have thirteen dead men, three of whom are actually dead, two who are in custody and-what?-eight who aren't dead?"

"Possibly," Anthony said, rubbing his chin. "We won't know until we actually identify them all, though."

"Or we get some answers from our pals back at the bank." Fowler said, "Who owned the rig?"

Anthony looked at him. "Who else? Harold Oliver Graybuck. He bought these monuments for every town that lost someone in the explosion."

"Awful friendly of him," Fowler said.

"The question is, what does this have to do with the robberies?" Anthony said.

"I really hate mysteries," Fowler said.

"So you said," Anthony said.

"I felt like reiterating," Fowler said, rubbing the back of his neck. "Do you think Annie Sanders knew about Graybuck's connection to these banks?"

"Yes," Anthony said. "According to Harry, she was a precocious kid. Smart for her age. He started her education early."

"Business education, you mean?"

"Yes. And I think we can certainly say that these men are responsible for her kidnapping now."

"Dead men." Fowler shook his head. "So this is what-revenge?"

"That's the theory I'm working under."

Fowler blinked. "Thirteen for thirteen. Put to proof his high supremacy." He snapped his fingers. "Thirteen banks for thirteen men." He looked at Anthony. "Graybuck's in Chicago, right?"

"Yes," Anthony said. His eyes widened suddenly. "They're going after Graybuck!"

"That's the theory *I'm* working under," Fowler said, tapping his brow with a finger. "Chicago is about four hours away. Think that souped-up Rolls of yours has enough juice left in it to make it?"

"We'll see, won't we?"

As they headed back, Fowler snagged one of the officers. "They caught the one who legged it?"

The cop shook his head. "Looks like he turned off on one of the back roads and somebody was waiting to pick him up. When our people got there, the car was on fire and there was no sign of the driver."

"That's the MO," Fowler said, looking at Anthony. He turned back to the cop. "Get your chief to get on the horn with the Chicago branch of the Bureau when he gets back. Have him send some guys down to take those two wing-nuts into-"

"Hey!" the other cop yelped. Fowler and Anthony spun as the restrained robber, Blum, began to thrash and squirm.

"Damn it!" Anthony bounded forward. Fowler rushed past him to check on the other captive. Unfortunately, Tom Hitch was already dead, his body contorted grotesquely. His cuffed hands were pressed against his head, and Fowler knew instantly that Hitch had snapped his own neck.

A slow hiss of sound slipped out of Fowler's lips as he contemplated the dead man. Cold fury filled him, and his hands curled into fists. He stalked out of the bank. "Is he dead?"

"He's trying his best," Anthony said, standing up, his hands covered in blood. "He tried to chew off his own tongue, just like Brackett."

"What'd you do?"

"I broke his jaw in three places," Anthony said curtly. He pointed a bloody finger at one of the cops, who grimaced squeamishly. "Get the local sawbones. This man needs to be restrained and sedated right now."

"Will he make it?" Fowler said.

"No clue," Anthony said pulling a handkerchief out of his pocket and wiping his hands clean. "Regardless, he won't be talking for awhile. The other-"

"Dead."

Anthony tossed his head in evident irritation. "We need to get to Chicago. If you're right, they'll be going after Graybuck next."

"I am." Fowler chewed his lip. "We need to alert Chicago field office. See if they can send some agents to meet us."

"The radio in the car should still be working," Anthony said, gesturing to the car. The Rolls was battered, but unbroken. Anthony slapped the hood as he moved towards the driver's side. "I made some structural improvements a while back, for certain situations. Reinforced the framework. Bullet-proof windows."

"Must be nice to be rich," Fowler said, getting in. Leaving a crime scene behind was irksome, but time was of the essence. He let his gaze linger on the bodies, and the fury nestled comfortably in his breast.

"Nice to be smart, too," Anthony said, throwing the car into gear.

"You think a bit highly of yourself, don't you?"

"Your reputation as an investigator is sadly oversold if you're just now figuring that out." Anthony grinned.

Fowler gave a sharp laugh. "Chicago, Jeeves."

"Right away, sir."

The Rolls gave a grumble and they left Denville. At Anthony's direction, Fowler flipped a catch on the dashboard and a hidden radio set descended.

"If we had a fraction of your budget," Fowler said, unhooking the microphone.

"You do, actually," Anthony said. "But I'm always available for consultation."

"Oh the Director would just love that," Fowler said.

"Sarcasm, Inspector?"

"Statement of fact." Fowler cycled through the signal settings until he reached the correct frequency. Under the Director's orders, Fowler had overseen the installation of radio receivers in every branch office in the United States, and his encyclopedic memory held tight to each of those frequencies.

The Chicago office, unfortunately, wasn't answering. Fowler looked at Anthony. "Police band?"

"Try frequency six," Anthony said. "If nothing else, we'll be able to eavesdrop."

Fowler spun the dial and a squawk of white noise greeted them. Voice tumbled over one another in a cacophony of sound. "Something is going on," Fowler said.

"Keep cycling through," Anthony said, his face set into grim lines.

They rode in silence, save for the bursts of noise echoing from the radio. Finally, Fowler found a strong signal. A radio announcer's voice uttered breathless words of terror.

"-unmen are rampaging through Chicago's Merchandise Mart! The world's largest building-so large that it has its own post office-is now a scene of bloody chaos as an unknown number of masked individuals issue bizarre demands from-"

"Frequency twelve," Anthony said. "Military frequency," he continued, catching Fowler's questioning look. Fowler flipped the switch.

"-rigged to explode, they say. From what I can tell, they're giving it to us straight-" The voice devolved into static.

"Too much chatter," Anthony said. "The Merchandise Mart." He shook his head. "I can't believe it."

Fowler looked at Anthony. "They wouldn't. There's no benefit to it!"

"I think they know that," Anthony said. "It stands to reason. Everything they've done so far has been planned with almost military precision, carried out by men who, whether consciously or no, are willing to sacrifice themselves for the overall goal. Sacrificing a few of their own to distract the law enforcement community is small potatoes."

"This can't be about the money," Fowler said. "Not entirely."

"Maybe." Anthony shook himself all over. "Regardless, we can't do anything about it. We need to get to Graybuck."

"They must really hate this guy," Fowler said. "All this, just to punish him."

"Things are rarely as simple as they seem, Inspector."

"Bull-puckey. Things are always as simple as they seem. It's people who complicate things." Fowler looked out the window. "Follow the money, follow the woman, and follow the grudge." He rapped his knuckles against the window. "We're three for three."

"But why kill themselves?" Anthony said. "Why the Milton on the walls? And why haven't they issued a ransom demand for Annie Sanders?"

"The Milton is easy," Fowler said. "It's a statement of intent. They want us to know why they're doing what they're doing. Revenge isn't the same without an audience."

"Possibly. It doesn't sit well in my little gray cells, however."

"Little gray cells?"

"A phrase I picked up from a friend in Belgium. What would wildcatters know from Milton?" Anthony said.

"Poor people read too, Anthony," Fowler said.

"Yes, but Milton?"

"Put the Milton aside for a minute." Fowler frowned. "If there was no ransom demand, how did Graybuck know his kid had been kidnapped?"

"It-ah." Anthony's eyes seemed to light up. "I read about it in the papers, but when I questioned Harry, he said there had been no demand."

"And you didn't think that was pertinent?"

"Not at the time," Anthony said. "The Graybucks have weathered kidnappings before. Annie was taken twice when she was a young girl, once in the Sudan, and once in Brazil. I didn't think it was that strange."

"Remind me not to get adopted by a tycoon," Fowler said. "So why is this time any different?"

"Because this time, I'm the one investigating."

"Didn't sit well in the little gray cells?" Fowler said.

"No." Anthony tapped the brake, slowing the Rolls. "Graybuck's estate is coming up. He lives just outside of the city."

"Likes his privacy, hunh?"

"Most wealthy men do." Anthony pulled the car off of the road. "How do you feel about insurance?"

"Depends. Is it the type that pays for the funeral, or the type that keeps me from having to have one?"

"The latter, in this case." Anthony leaned his seat back and reached up, stripping away a false panel on the inside of the Rolls' roof. A set of thin metal cuirasses were revealed, held in place by straps. Anthony popped the straps and pulled two of the odd vests down. He dropped one in Fowler's lap. "Bullet-proof," he said.

"This car is a regular rolling armory," Fowler said.

"Always be prepared, my father taught me."

"Smart man."

Anthony grunted. He and Fowler struggled into the vests, hiding them beneath their shirts. Then they got back on the road.

"You think he's involved?" Fowler said, after a while.

"I hope not."

"But just in case-"

"Don't mention the vests," Anthony said grimly.

The Graybuck estate wasn't the sprawling monstrosity Fowler had half-expected. It was a tastefully designed country house in the English style, with a number of out-buildings and a nice empty lawn all the way around.

As they drove towards the front, they saw a number of men, dressed casually, but carrying rifles, moving through the grounds.

"He's got a damn army," Fowler murmured. "Why are we worried about him again?"

"We're not. We're worried about a missing girl," Anthony said.

"Except you don't really think she's missing," Fowler said.

Anthony shot him a look. "What?"

"You heard me. You as much said that you thought the kidnapping was faked."

"No. What I intimated was that Harry tried to send me in the wrong direction, knowingly or otherwise." Anthony took the car around the drive.

"Same thing," Fowler said. "If Graybuck is involved, the girl likely isn't missing."

"And if he's not?"

"Then there was a ransom demand, and he didn't tell you about it," Fowler said sharply as he got out of the car. "Either way, we're figuring this out today."

They moved towards the front doors of the house even as the portal in question was opened as if to admit them.

The man on the other side of the door looked like a snake and dressed like a butler. All thin limbs and languid movements. "Mr. Anthony," he said, staring down his nose at them. "Mr. Graybuck is in his office. This way, if you please."

Fowler looked at Anthony as they followed the butler, and made a surreptitious gesture. There was an indistinct bulge just under the butler's left arm, and he moved with the slightest of lists, both of which were sure signs that the man was armed.

Anthony nodded tersely and made a gesture to indicate that he'd seen the same thing. Fowler subsided.

Graybuck's office was equal parts library and boardroom. A vaulted ceiling, covered in a massive mural depicting a great orange predatory cat in the streets of some Italian city, looked down on dark hardwood floors and ceiling to floor bookshelves. On the second floor, the office looked out over the grounds and a large greenhouse. Graybuck was reputed to be a fan of orchids.

Graybuck himself stood with his back to the door, staring out the window behind his desk. The desk was piled high with books and ledgers. Fowler's keen eyes picked out a familiar title or two, and the tumblers in his head began to click. As they entered, a dumpy-looking man in an ill-fitting blue suit waved a handful of papers at Graybuck in distress. Graybuck waved a hand and turned.

"Enough, Dithers. I am quite aware of the value of our stock at the moment. Now, I have another appointment. Please see yourself out."

Graybuck was tall, broad and glaringly bald. Pale, intense eyes swept over Anthony first, then over Fowler. They lingered on the Federal agent for a moment, then shifted back to Anthony.

"Jim. Have you found her?" he said.

"No. I'm sorry, Harry." Anthony stopped a few feet from the desk, his hands behind his back. Behind them, Dithers left the office and closed the doors behind him.

Graybuck's face didn't change. "Have you found anything?"

"They're hitting your banks," Fowler said, taking his hat off and slapping it against his leg. "And they worked for you."

"And you are?"

"Fowler. Inspector Daniel Fowler, FBI." Fowler held up his badge. "I'd like to ask you a few questions, if I may."

"Jim?" Graybuck said.

"Harry, answer his questions." Anthony crossed his arms. "It could help us find Annie."

Graybuck hesitated, but then nodded briskly. "Fine. Ask away."

"Do the names Brackett, Blum or Hitch ring any bells for you?"

"No. Can't say that they do."

"That's funny. You built thirteen monuments with their names displayed prominently on them." Fowler leaned over the desk, teeth bared.

Graybuck blinked. Then said, "The Crawford Rig Explosion."

"Give the man a prize," Fowler said, pulling his cigarette case out of his coat. He plucked one out and lit it.

"I cannot abide the smell of cigarettes," Graybuck said.

"And I can't abide the sound of lies," Fowler said. A moment later, a brown hand snatched the cigarette from between his lips moments later, and crushed it out with a single, imperious gesture.

Fowler spun. "Who the-"

"My man, Khyber," Graybuck said, motioning to the large man who had appeared as if from nowhere. Tall, even more so than Anthony and Fowler, and imposingly built, Khyber was dressed in a tastefully tailored suit and a neatly wrapped turban. Dark eyes glared at Fowler from over a hawk-like nose.

"I didn't hear him come in," Anthony said.

"Khyber is experienced in the business of silence," Graybuck said, smiling slightly. "Now, I believe you were accusing me of something?"

"Yeah. I guess you don't remember the names of the men who died to make you rich," Fowler said. It wasn't a fair shot, but Fowler was annoyed. Graybuck was entirely too composed for a man whose daughter was missing and whose wallet had just been hit thirteen times in a row.

"A low blow, Inspector. I'll have you know that I'm an acquaintance of your Director-"

"How about that? Me too," Fowler said. "Getting back on the subject, it looks like you got a problem with ghosts."

Graybuck blinked, thrown. "What?"

"Ghosts. Dead men walking. Dead men wearing masks," Fowler said, pulling the folded up metal mask he'd taken off of Blum out of his coat pocket. He tossed it onto Graybuck's desk. "Those banks of yours-"

"I don't own any banks," Graybuck said.

Anthony cleared his throat. "Hate to disagree with you, Harry."

"What?"

"I looked into some things."

"You invaded my privacy?"

"To find your daughter," Anthony said. "Besides, detective, remember?"

"Those funds were donations!" Graybuck said.

"But they weren't really, were they?" Fowler said. "You were playing it cagey, like any good tycoon. Using the banks to hide funds you didn't want the tax man taking a bite out of. That's what they were after."

"The ghosts you mean?" Graybuck said, smiling slightly.

"Yeah." Fowler gestured to the mask.

"They kidnapped your daughter because of those banks, Harry," Anthony said. Graybuck's eyes widened.

"But the evidence-Saint Sebastian-you said-"

"You told me yourself that she had access to the records of every business transaction you had ever made," Anthony went on.

"But-"

"But nothing. They took the girl and began hitting banks a week a later. Your banks. Just yours. That's the pattern." Fowler snapped his fingers at the mask. "The question I got, is why?"

"Why? Why what?" Graybuck said, sitting down heavily.

"Why you? Why are they after you? What happened on that oil rig that set thirteen ghosts on your trail, Graybuck. Thirteen men willing to die to punch you in the money-belt. And why did they wait two years after the fact?"

Graybuck turned away, saying nothing. Fowler leaned over the desk, balancing on his knuckles. "Answer me damn it!"

Khyber stepped up to him, head cocked. He grabbed Fowler's shoulder and easily jerked him away from the desk. Fowler turned, and froze. Khyber's eyes blazed and Fowler felt a strange, but familiar weakness curl through him. He stumbled back, until Anthony put out a hand to stop him.

"What?" he said.

"Nothing. Just tired, I think," Fowler said, shaking his head, remembering the confrontation in the barn and the turban they'd found. Khyber frowned at them, his big hands curling into knotted fists.

"Did you come here just to accuse me of misdeeds, Jim?" Graybuck said, without turning around.

"No. We came to save your life," Anthony said.

Graybuck turned, eyes narrowed. "My life?"

"This will go faster if you stop repeating everything I say," Jim said. "Yes, your life. Thirteen men hit thirteen banks. They took your money and kidnapped your ward. And now, in all likelihood, they're coming for you."

Graybuck went pale. He glanced at Khyber. The big man nodded and headed for the door. Graybuck looked back at Fowler and Anthony. "Thank you, gentlemen. I appreciate your timely warning. Now, if you'll excuse me-"

"Whoa, hold up there chief," Fowler said. "We're not going anywhere. The minute your pals in the masks decided to hit a bank, this became a Federal matter. And as the only representative of the Federal government here, I'm staying."

"I assure you that my men and I are fully capable of-" Graybuck began, rising to his feet.

"Bupkiss," Fowler said, grinning savagely. "Besides which, they've tried to kill me twice now. That's interfering and assault on a Federal Agent in the pursuit of his duties. Can't have that, can we?"

"No, I suppose not," Graybuck said slowly.

"Sir?"

All three men turned. The butler stood in the doorway, his face a stiff

"…the large man appeared as if from nowhere."

mask of concern. "The perimeter guards have not called to check in."

Anthony looked at Fowler. "They're here."

"Good," Fowler said. "Get Graybuck to safety."

"And you?"

"I'm going to do my job." Fowler flicked the brim of his hat and looked at Graybuck. "You hunt?"

"I have a display case of firearms in the lounge, if that's what you're asking," Graybuck said. "Mostly antiques, but there are a few modern ones scattered throughout…"

"Good enough. You, come with me," Fowler barked, gesturing to the butler. The latter glanced at Graybuck, who, after a long moment, nodded.

The butler led Fowler to the lounge, and gestured to the large display case near the fireplace. Fowler opened the case and ran a finger across the row of weapons. He plucked a well-tended M-1 carbine out of its place and checked the ammunition clip.

"This'll do. You know how to use that gat, pal?" he said, pointing at the bulge beneath the butler's coat.

The butler's hand flashed up, patting his coat. "I'm well-versed in the shootist's art, sir."

"Got a name?"

"Asper."

Fowler nodded. "Asper, I'm Fowler. Do what I say and maybe we both make it out of this alive and well."

"I intend to do so, sir."

"Right. Which side of the house faces the perimeter you were talking about?"

Before the butler could answer, the house trembled to its ancient foundations, and the sound of splintering wood and shattering glass filled the air. Fowler turned, sweeping the carbine up. "Never mind," he said. "Sounds like the fight just came to us."

"Indeed." Asper pulled his pistol and racked the slide in one sinuous motion. Then, with barely a hint of further movement, he shot Fowler twice in the back.

Fowler stumbled, breath whooshing out of his lungs as the twin hammer blows sent him sprawling. The carbine spun out of his grip and he fell flat.

He fought the urge to get to his feet and instead lay still, playing dead. Anthony's bulletproof vest had done its job, keeping him from being perforated, but it still felt like someone had swung a chunk of rebar against his spine.

Asper stepped over him, pistol pressed against his leg. "Is it done?" he called out. Khyber stepped into the room, dusting his hands together. The big man nodded, his eyes glittering weirdly. Fowler kept his eyes narrowed to slits and his body limp.

"Good. Have the others arrived?"

Another nod. Asper chuckled. "Excellent. Mr. Graybuck will reward us both well, my friend."

Graybuck? Fowler restrained a twitch, forcing himself not to move. Like the tumblers in a safe, facts began to slot into place.

"Him?" Asper said, catching Fowler's attention. "He's no longer an issue. Likely they'll pin a medal on his headstone." The butler chuckled dryly. "I'm sure he'd have enjoyed that. He seemed the type."

Asper and Khyber left the room, leaving him to rot. Or so they thought. Fowler took a shallow breath and counted to ten, then pushed himself to his feet. Stretching slightly to work out the kinks in his back and arms, Fowler trotted towards the door. Along the way he scooped up the carbine.

Pressing his ear to the door, Fowler listened. Booted feet struck the floor of the hallway. Hobnails. The rustle of cheap fabric. The rasp of metal.

As the sounds faded, Fowler pulled open the door and stepped out. He moved as silently as possible down the hall, rifle held ready.

Several steps from the office doors, he heard a woman's voice. Fowler froze.

"Do you think he's alive?"

"Doubtful. I shot him twice, and the fall out the window would certainly handle the rest." That was Graybuck. Fowler bared his teeth. He and Anthony had been played.

"I don't see him," the woman said.

"He fell into the greenhouse. It's of no matter. The body will be obliterated either way when the house goes."

"Whatever you say, Daddy."

"You have performed admirably, Annie," Graybuck said. "Of course, there is still one remaining task before we take our leave. Khyber, Asper. If you please."

The roar of an automatic rifle sent Fowler ducking for cover. Wooden splinters flew, chewed free of the wall by what Fowler's trained ear thought were .30-06 cartridges. It took him only a few seconds to realize that he hadn't been the target.

"There now. The last of our sad dupes are dead in a suicidal attack on my estate, which resulted in an unfortunate explosion, killing all inside."

"It's a tragedy, Daddy."

Scrambling to his feet, Fowler charged the door to the office and took it off the hinges with his shoulder. He rolled across the floor, swinging the carbine up to take aim at a point somewhere between Graybuck's pale eyes.

"Nobody move!" Fowler said.

"Daddy-" a crimson haired woman dressed in a loose boiler suit yelped, raising a Mauser as she bolted off of Graybuck's desk like a scalded cat.

"Sweetheart, you even twitch and I will preemptively defend myself," Fowler snapped, casting a quick glance around the room. Khyber stood near the wall, a Browning automatic rifle clutched in his big hands. The

BAR was still smoking from the barrage that had put paid to the lives of the five masked men lying in a tangled heap, their blood creating red rivers across the floor. Opposite that gruesome scene, the great window that looked out over the estate was broken.

Asper was staring at him in undisguised shock, and Fowler grinned. "I'm ready for that medal now, Asper."

"Sir, I-" Asper began, looking at Graybuck.

Graybuck gestured with the pistol he still held. "It's not important. Mr. Fowler, surely you see that-"

"Inspector Fowler," Fowler said "And I see a lot of things." He glanced at the bodies. "Like those poor saps."

"A necessary evil, I'm afraid," Graybuck said.

"They were willing to die for you."

"Amazing what two years of intensive sleep deprivation and hypnosis will do when applied correctly," Annie said, circling Fowler, the Mauser extended. "Ol' Khyber is a dab eye with that sub-continental hoodoo-"

"Annie!" Graybuck barked.

"Let her talk, Graybuck," Fowler said, remembering the feeling that had rushed through him when Khyber had stared at him. The big man had been the one in the barn. He'd met a Svengali or two in his career, but the big Indian took the cake. "I may as well hear your confession while we wait for the locals."

"You didn't call anyone," Graybuck said, smiling slightly. "I made sure the eyes of every local law enforcement agent would be elsewhere."

"Except me."

"Except you," Graybuck said softly. "Unfortunate, but even the best strategies require battlefield adaptation sometimes."

"So why call in Anthony?"

"Fog of war," Graybuck said. "Jim was a better detective than I thought. And Annie was…careless."

"How was I to know that stupid cow behind the counter would pull off my hat?" Annie said. "I fixed her for it though!"

"And why were you wearing a hat in the first place?" Graybuck snapped. Annie flinched back, lip trembling.

"Let me kill him, sir. I'll make it stick this time," Asper said. Khyber raised his BAR.

"Feel free to try, chum," Fowler said. "But are you quick enough to plug me before I plug your boss?"

"I am," Annie said.

Fowler looked at her. "Guess you weren't kidnapped after all, hunh?"

"Not even close. Daddy needed somebody he could trust in charge of things-"

"Annie, be quiet," Graybuck said. "Inspector, this little standoff won't solve anything. No one is coming. And in roughly twenty minutes, this fine house will be immolated. As will we, if we're still here."

"I'm willing to take that chance," Fowler said, cutting his eyes towards the window. He thought he'd caught a glimpse of something there. He smiled and turned his full attention back to Graybuck. "So what was it, really? The money? Was this just some convoluted embezzlement scheme?"

"I see it as taking back what's mine," Graybuck said.

"So, you engineer a mining disaster in order to put together a crew of dead men to rob your banks for your money, so you can-what?" Fowler cocked his head. "Put to proof your high supremacy?"

Graybuck flinched as if Fowler had pulled the trigger. Fowler's smile went as thin as a knife blade. "Yeah. Yeah I had you pegged for that sort right off, Graybuck. You *wanted* people to know. Fog of war, my Aunt Petunia. You called in Anthony just to see if you could get away with it. Robbery is a good way to disappear money, but you could have had Asper or Khyber there do the job with a bunch of Chicago bagmen. But you wanted to make it a game. Proof of your supremacy, right?" Fowler jerked his chin towards the desk and the copy of Milton still visible on it. "You read your Milton wrong, though."

"Oh?" Graybuck said.

"Yeah, Satan failed, remember?"

"Quiet!" Annie snapped, stomping towards him. "No one talks about Daddy that way!"

"Ms. Annie, don't get in the line of fire!" Asper barked.

Two things happened at once. The Mauser spoke, and something shrieked and hurled itself through the broken window.

Fowler felt the burn of the bullet across the surface of his cheek even as he fired the carbine. Graybuck gave a howl of pain and fell backwards. Annie spun towards him, screaming. Fowler stepped forward, flinging the carbine at Asper. The gunman hopped back, right into the arms of the black shape that vaulted off of Graybuck's desk.

Anthony, his feet bare and the sleeves of his sweater riding up over his corded forearms like a child's outfit, spun Asper into the air and brought him crashing down against the floor. The Super-Detective hauled the man up as easily as a gorilla and drove him into Khyber, who was trying to line the BAR up for a shot. The two killers fell in a tangle.

"Glad to see I bought you enough time to rejoin the party," Fowler said. "Took you long enough, though."

"You try climbing up a wall after getting two in the back," Anthony said, falling into a crouch as Khyber struggled to his feet. "Did you put the time to good use, at least?"

"I got a confession or three, yes."

"Maybe there's a detective in you yet, Inspector," Anthony said. Khyber lunged for him, groping for his throat then and the two big men crashed together a moment later.

Fowler turned even as Annie lunged for him, the Mauser extended. He brought his arm up, swatting the pistol aside, and drove a fist into her gut. She doubled over, gasping. "Sorry lady. Chivalry takes a backseat to not getting shot."

Her fist shot out, and Fowler gave a wheeze as pain shot through his lower extremities. He fell, and Annie dropped onto him, her fingers digging for his eyes.

"Get off of me you hell-cat!" Fowler groaned, catching her in the belly with his knees and throwing her aside. He rolled to his feet, and some instinct warned him to weave to the side. A pistol barked and Annie, back on her feet, gasped.

Fowler twisted around, clouting Graybuck across the jaw. The bald man's head snapped back and he toppled across the desk, the pistol falling from his limp fingers. Fowler turned, eyes searching.

Annie Sanders was curled into a ball on the floor, a slow pool of red spreading outward from her. Fowler dropped to his knees, cursing. He pushed the woman over, then ripped off his jacket and tore out the lining. He pressed it to the wound in her belly. She groaned.

He heard the click of a cocking mechanism, but didn't turn. "You shoot me, Asper, and there's a good chance she dies," he said.

"That's an acceptable risk," Asper hissed.

"Not to me. Put it down," Anthony said. Fowler glanced over as Anthony lifted the BAR and stepped over Khyber's unconscious form. "Drop the pistol, or I'll drop you."

"That thing will chew us all up," Asper laughed. "Go ahead, if you don't mind chopping the G-Man into bits along with me."

"Man's right," Fowler said mildly.

"I suppose," Anthony said, shrugging. Then he swiftly reversed his grip on the automatic rifle and swung it like a baseball bat. The rifle connected with the butler's jaw and Asper spun like a top before crashing to the ground, his head angled oddly.

Anthony tossed the BAR aside and came over. "Is she-"

"Close. Got a medical degree in that bag of tricks of yours?"

"I've got a battlefield doctorate," Anthony said, dropping to his haunches. "What about the butler?"

"Pretty sure you killed him, Sherlock. And good riddance." Fowler rose to his feet and stalked towards the desk. Graybuck stirred as Fowler's shadow fell over him. Fowler grabbed Graybuck by his lapels and jerked the bald man to his feet.

"I calculate that we've got less than ten minutes left before this house goes boom. Give me a reason not to leave you behind."

"Money," Graybuck hissed between clenched teeth. His pale eyes were wide with pain. "I'll pay you-"

"Wrong answer," Fowler said. "But I forgive you. Besides, there's no reason you should get off so easy-"

Two big hands fastened on either side of Fowler's head and he found himself hurling backwards, into the wall. Plaster cracked at the force of impact, and he fell in a shower of dust. Khyber hauled Graybuck to his feet and hefted the wounded man, his terrifying eyes flashing like sour lightning.

"Not so fast, pal," Fowler said, clambering to his feet. "We've still got to finish our little dance from the barn before..." His voice died in his throat as Khyber's eyes met his. Fowler felt that strange weakness again, the sense that switches in his brain were being flicked. He hesitated, unable to focus.

"Fowler!" Anthony's voice sounded as if it were coming through a wall of water. He shook his head, trying to focus. Khyber's stare seemed to intensify, and he felt his soul peeling back, layer by layer.

Was this what they had felt? The Crawford thirteen, trapped in some hole somewhere, programmed into being murderers? Two years of being stripped down, one thought at a time by this silent demon?

Strength flooded him as he thought of them. Of the people they had been forced to kill. All so one greedy man could keep his hands clean.

"No. No, I got this," Fowler said, his mouth feeling as if it were full of cotton, and he lowered his head and charged. Khyber blinked but didn't move quick enough to avoid Fowler's headlong rush. The desk was knocked over as all three men went down.

Graybuck yowled and clutched at his arm as he tried to kick his way free. Fowler grabbed his ankle with one hand and used his other to jerk his pistol out of his coat. Khyber rose up off of the floor like a tidal wave, beard bristling. His eyes seemed to glow with an eerie light and they opened wider than seemed possible.

Fowler shot him three times. Khyber took a step back with every shot until the backs of his knees connected with the window-sill. He stood there for a moment, swaying, his mouth working soundlessly. His eyes had become dull, black marbles.

Fowler remembered Brackett chewing off his own tongue, and Hitch snapping his own neck. Lifting the pistol, he fired again, and Khyber pitched backwards, out of the window.

The house shook as something deep in its bowels exploded. Fowler climbed to his feet and jerked Graybuck up, holding his hands pinned behind his back.

"We need to get out of here," Anthony said, picking up the woman. "Can you carry him?"

"I think I can manage. Let's go."

Two more explosions ripped through the guts of the house as they moved, showering them all with plaster, splinters and dust.

Outside, they watched as the Graybuck estate collapsed in on itself. Graybuck, his face ashen, was unceremoniously dropped to the ground by Fowler. "The girl?"

Anthony, kneeling over Annie, said, "She'll live, if I can stabilize her. There's a first-aid kit under the floorboard in the back of the Rolls."

"Of course there is," Fowler said as he retrieved it. Tossing the metal box to Anthony, he sank to his haunches in front of Graybuck, who was staring at the burning wreckage of his estate with something resembling shock. "Don't worry about the house, Graybuck, because you'll be getting a brand new six by eight apartment all to yourself."

"I won't spend a day in jail. You have no evidence!" Graybuck spat, pulling himself into a sitting position. "You broke into MY home, killed MY employees and blew up MY house! I'm the victim here!" His smile was ghastly. "In fact, I think I'll be having your badge very soon, *Inspector* Fowler."

Hands dangling between his knees, Fowler nodded along with Graybuck's words. Then, "It took your pet Svengali two years to break thirteen men down and turn them into killers and thieves. How long do you think it'll take us to bring just one of them out of it?"

Graybuck's face assumed the consistency of wax as he took in the implications of Fowler's statement. "But-but you said-"

"I didn't say anything of the sort." Fowler stood and pulled his cigarette case out of his pocket. "Of course, if you'd read your Milton a little more closely, you'd have known this wasn't going to work. Satan might have tested God, but he still lost." Fowler turned. "He lost his home, his power, and his followers." He blew a plume of smoke into the air, where it mingled with the black smoke rising from the inferno. "The irony is, Satan set out to prove his own superiority, but in the end, he only proved God's."

Graybuck said nothing. He simply slumped, his face blank. Fowler, cigarette dangling from his lips, turned to Anthony.

"Well?"

"If we get her to the hospital in the next two hours, she'll live to stand trial," Anthony said, rubbing bloody fingers across his sweater. "Not a bad day's work, I have to say." He looked at the fire and then at Fowler. "Thanks for your help, Inspector. Or, rather, thanks for letting me help." Anthony smiled, the hard planes of his face softening. Fowler looked at him for a moment, deciding.

Then, he extended his hand. "Call me Dan."

The End

First we Fight, Then we Team-up (Part One)

I'm a sucker for a good team-up.

Case in point-one of my most prized possessions is a ratty copy of *Marvel Two-in-One* issue 21, in which the ever-lovin' blue-eyed Idol of Millions, the Thing, teams up with the Man of Bronze, Doc Savage. It's not really a great story, but the concept was aces.

Team-ups, people. They're awesome, even if they kind of suck. But we don't see many out and out team-ups (or crossovers, if you prefer) in pulp prose. Prose is a different beast than comics and unless your name is Phillip Jose Farmer or Fred Saberhagen you probably aren't going to play mix-n-match with the fruits of pulpdom's proverbial looms.

I apologize for that last bit of undergarment themed humor. Back to my point (he has a point?) we need more team-ups. I mean, I know the Black Coat Press boys are holding up their end of things, and the gentlemen from the Wold of Newton have charted relationships where no relationships dared tread before, but come on...there's no rights issues here. These are all public domain characters. No pesky copyrights or shared worlds getting in the way. Why can't the Green Lama pit his mystic might against the machinations of Dr. Satan? Why can't the Moon Man steal a valuable and dangerous thingamumy from Jim Anthony's Penthouse (that idea's mine by the by, and I'll thank you to keep your grubby mitts off of it)? And Dan Fowler certainly tried to arrest the Black Bat during the Siege of Coney Island, right?

So, that's why I wrote this story about the (possible) first (but certainly not only) meeting between G-Man and Super-Detective. It's an odd fit, to say the least. On the face of it, the two characters are remarkably similar. But it's only a surface similarity...Dan Fowler is Melvin Purvis without the sense of humor and Jim Anthony is Nick Charles with a tan. One is a solid proponent of law and order, the other a man who often indulges in a more natural justice.

It's more than just the difference between the professional and the amateur. Fowler is a blue collar man, and likely wasn't on (and certainly didn't approve of) Hoover's union-busting squads. Anthony is a philanthropist and a tycoon. The one hunts men because it's his job, the other because he wants to. Anthony is a thrill-seeker, a dilettante and a law unto himself. Fowler is a representative of Uncle Sam, a by the book lawman who memorized the Constitution AND the Articles of the Confederation just to be on the safe side.

Two characters with vastly different methods of obtaining the same goal. It writes itself, it really does. And it did.

I am, however, proud to say that I did not succumb to the temptation outlined in this essay's title. There's no fight before the team-up. It doesn't really make sense, after all, for two such straight-arrows to go at it tooth and nail.

Besides, I had to save SOMETHING for the Jim Anthony/Black Bat team-up...but that's another essay.

JOSHUA M.REYNOLDS - is a freelance writer of moderate skill and exceptional confidence. He has written a bit, and some of it was even published. For money. By real people. His work has appeared in anthologies such as *Cthulhu Unbound 2*, and in periodicals such as *Innsmouth Free Press*.

Feel free to stop by his blog, [http://joshuamreynolds.blogspot.com/] and cast aspersions on his character.

in

"Feasting on the Predator's Corpse"
by
B.C. Bell

New York 1927

Growing up, Charles Dudka had never had much of a family life. Probably because he'd never had much of a family. When his dad wasn't battling the bottle, he was battling the rest of the family. And the bottle always won.

The only thing worse than the senior Dudka's drunken rages were his dry ones. The ones where he beat his wife's face in with his fists, locked Chuck's sister in the closet, and broke more bones than anybody would ever care to remember—until finally the money for booze was put into his hands.

Then, after a half-bottle's worth of peace, "Pop" would sense the need to start the whole process all over again. Chuck's mom found a solution in prayer. It might have helped her, but it didn't help the kids.

New to both America and Brooklyn, Chuck hadn't grown up with the rest of the kids in the neighborhood, so he kept to himself. To the casual observer, he looked like a serious, responsible young man. He didn't hang out in pool halls, or sit out on the stoop, smoking and harassing passersby like those "no-good kids down the block."

In fact, his cultural differences and shy demeanor made him a tourist in his own neighborhood. He went to school. He wasn't in a gang. And he couldn't have palled around with the neighborhood kids if he'd wanted to. You would think it would have kept him out of trouble.

It didn't.

Never knowing what he might face when he went home, Chuck simply didn't go. He'd started off taking long walks, anything to just not be in the house. He had a pretty good sense of direction, always knowing which way he was headed even in a strange part of the city. Until one day, his feet got tired.

That was the day Chuck Dudka stole his first car. He'd read in a true-crime magazine how to do it, and had been contemplating the crime for awhile. He drove around for almost three hours, then parked the stolen car several blocks from his house. When he got home, his dad had already passed out for the night.

It was as if that first joyride had set him free.

Pretty soon, Chuck was stealing a car a week just for the feeling of freedom it granted him. He hadn't figured out who he could sell the hot vehicles to yet, and, while he could use the money, it wasn't the money he was becoming addicted to. It was the rush of being on his own; answerable to only himself, that fueled his newfound freedom. It was the first time in his life he had ever felt like he was in control. He liked that feeling. Confidence. It changed him. Even on the prowl he walked tall.

It was on just such a dry, brown, autumn night that Chuck Dudka found an entirely new calling, something life changing. He'd stolen an old Model-A Ford and taken it for a spin around the city, committing every random street to the almost perfect map of the boroughs in his mind. After waiting a sufficient amount of time for his father to pass out, Chuck parked the car eight blocks away, hopped a streetcar and began walking home. But, to get back home, Chuck had to walk past the Carbone brothers' house.

No reference to "no-good kids sitting on the stoop, harassing innocent passersby" would have been complete without the inclusion of the Carbone brothers' little gang. Chuck had already been through his share of beatings from the boys. Alone, he hadn't stood a chance. So on this evening, when Vinnie Carbone once again called him a "stinkin' Polack," he tried to ignore it and just walk by.

Vinnie threw a bottle at him. It missed and shattered in the street. Vinnie grabbed Chuck by the collar as the kid turned to run.

"I don't wanna see you on my street, Dudka!" Carbone threatened. "You wanna get home you gotta pay the toll."

Chuck stood still, staring back in Vinnie's eyes, unsure of what to say.

"Half-wit," Vinnie said, and slapped him across the face.

Chuck's face flooded red, his visage pure rage. The Polish immigrant threw a right-cross out sheer frustration. Vinnie feinted to the left, and the blow glanced off part of his neck. He punched Chuck in the stomach. Chuck hunched over, clutching at his solar plexus, trying to force his breath back. He coughed, still not knowing what to say even if he could catch a lungful of air. Gasping, he shoved Vinnie away and lurched down the street.

When Chuck got home, none of the lights were on. Either his dad had passed out, or everybody was already hiding in their rooms—or both. *Good.* He climbed into his bedroom window, not wanting anybody to know he was home yet, because young Charles Dudka had come to a conclusion. Charles Dudka had decided Vinnie Carbone would never bother him again.

He would never have made the decision to fight back, if it hadn't been for the newfound confidence he'd gained stealing cars. No, he was through being the neighborhood punching bag. Chuck Dudka was the master of his own fate now. And nobody was ever going to laugh at him again.

Ten minutes later, Chuck was dressed completely in black and crawling out his bedroom window. Making his way down the back alley, he stopped next to a neighbor's coal bin. His empty hand reached inside, and came back out with a piece of iron pipe in it.

Vinnie Carbone was still loitering down the street, in the alley next to his tenement building, only a few feet from where he'd been before. Vinnie had bought a half-bucket of beer from a speakeasy, and stashed it behind the garbage cans next to the street. Using a jelly jar for a glass, he'd dip it into the little wooden pail, then step back out into the alley to smoke and drink.

It looked as if he were waiting for someone; so he didn't seem too surprised to hear somebody coming up the alley behind him. When he turned around and saw Chuck, his mouth curled into a demeaning smile. His head turned to-and-fro, tsk-tsking sarcastically.

"Yo, Polack! Didn't I tell you, you gotta pay the toll?" Then he saw the iron pipe hanging from Chuck's hand. "Hey, Dudka, don't do anything stupid. You know I'm just kidding, right?" Vinnie glanced over his shoulder, looking for help as he backed slowly toward the street.

He should never have even mentioned the possibility of Chuck being stupid. That was as bad as laughing at him.

Chuck's first swing broke one of Carbone's ribs and cracked two others. His second swing broke the cracked ones. The third was left-handed, but by then Carbone had fallen to the ground. Chuck didn't drop the pipe, but started kicking the folded body of his tormenter on the concrete.

The body went limp. Dudka just kept stomping.

When the rage's red veil finally parted, Chuck was kicking Vinnie in the head, and Carbone was face down on the concrete. Gasping, the young Pole wiped his brow with his forearm and stepped backward, almost collapsing into the brick wall behind him. Still struggling to catch his breath, he realized Vinnie wasn't. He grabbed the unconscious man's wrist and checked for a pulse. He hadn't meant to kill him, but Carbone was dead.

At first, Chuck panicked and started to run back home, but then—instantly—the fear melted away. He glanced up and down the street. It was night, nobody was around. He'd gotten lucky.

He knew he had to get rid of the body first—and fast. If he left it here in the alley, they'd start looking for the killer in the neighborhood. But if the body were to disappear...

He stashed Vinnie's body behind the garbage with the beer pail, and took the dead boys car keys out of his pocket. Then, casually, he walked down the block, opened and started Vinnie's car. Ten minutes later, Vinnie Carbone's body was in the trunk and headed upstate for a very private burial in the woods.

Chuck kept telling himself he hadn't meant to do it. They never should have picked on him. But, by the time he'd parked Vinnie's car and wiped it down for prints, he was feeling pretty good about it. In fact, taking the trolley home, the only thing that bothered him was that the murder didn't really bother him. *What was the big deal? Carbone had been asking for it.* By the time he was home again, Chuck realized he'd never felt better.

Within weeks he was walking from Bronx to Bowery, late at night with a knife hidden in his sleeve, perfecting his craft on drunks and panhandlers. Hunting.

1932

In his twenties, Dudka got a job as a construction worker, but quit when somebody offered him work collecting debts for a loan shark—collecting from the same men he'd been working with. Chuck had grown to be a large man, six-foot, four. It was an easy job for him, but he didn't suffer fools lightly. One day in a bar in Little Italy, while arguing with a mobster—who was determined *not* to pay another mobster—Chuck lost his patience. It was over fast, and—if he was lucky—the vindictive gangster on the bar stool *might* have seen Chuck pull a .38 out of his belt, he might even have felt the barrel slam against the side of his head, but the gun's meaning probably didn't register until a bullet popped out the other.

"He never knew what hit him," Chuck told a fellow torpedo.

And soon, he had a new job, working with "Happy" Malone and "Dasher" Abandando's crew from Ocean Hill. While Chuck was delighted to meet others as vicious as himself—particularly Malone, whose brandishing of a meat cleaver he admired—Dudka felt the Ocean Hill gang took too many risks. Striking in broad daylight and stirring up civilians wasn't good for business. And, though he wasn't above taking somebody out in a fit of rage, Chuck preferred his murder a little more subtle. He preferred to make it look like an accident if he could, or to make the body disappear completely.

After three successful assassinations together, Abandando asked Chuck if he wanted to make a little extra money. All he told the Polish immigrant was that "there was a man to be killed, here's where he lives, and he drives down the same dirt road every morning on his way to work." Chuck didn't care about the details; somebody needed to die.

For four days Dudka watched and waited. The victim seemed to live alone. Every morning he stepped outside and into a brand-new shiny Packard. Then, he'd pull out of his gated yard, lock it, and head down the road, dust kicking up behind him. On the fourth morning, the brand new car came around a bend in the road, and a bullet shattered its windshield.

The car veered hard left, still digging its way forward, off the road and into a ditch. Chuck came up out of a clump of bushes with a deer rifle. Going through the pockets of the victim, to confirm his kill, he found not only the dead man's driver's license but a badge: New York State Police # 2153.

Chuck knew he'd been set up. Not that he minded killing a cop, but they should have at least told him, so he'd be prepared. As it was, it could have been a lot worse; and it would be—for the Ocean Hill Gang.

Dudka bashed the policeman's skull to mush with a rock to destroy the head wound, then drove the car down the road to a cliff, and pushed it over with the policeman's body still inside.

That same night, he scheduled a meeting with Abandando in order to collect on the contract. Over drinks he brought up the fact that his last victim had been a cop.

"I thought I told you," Abandando said, trying to look as if he was remembering. "Or, maybe I didn't think you'd care, I dunno… Listen, I'm not going to be able to pay you until after the next job. You OK with that?"

"No, I did the job; you should be ready to pay. And next time tell me. I don't mind taking out a cop, just make sure I can take the proper precautions." He didn't mention that he knew he'd been set up. He knew they weren't going to pay him, they'd kill him first. They'd planned it so that either Chuck was going to take the fall for the murder, or, maybe, the gang just wanted something to hold over his head. It was one of the reasons Chuck didn't like working with other people, witnesses.

The gang's next big contract was in less than a week. Dutch Madigan, a low-rent, local gangster, had opened an unauthorized speakeasy on his own. He'd been paying off the cops—but not the organization. Chuck, "Dancer" Abandando, "Happy" Malone, and Tony "The Chin" Gregori were supposed to kill the owner and frighten the clientele away, all while razing the joint to the ground with gun fire and explosives.

Thursday night, the plan worked perfectly. Two men in the front door, two men in back. The Tommy guns terrorizing the crowd in front erupted. At the same time, one in back ripped off Madigan's head.

The gang emptied the club, blew the safe and emptied that, too. Then, with alibis already arranged, they drove to a Coney Island warehouse/garage that Abandando owned to hide out for the night. Normally after a job, the guys would be talking about how much the take was. Then, occasionally, somebody would try to negotiate for more. Sure, they'd already agreed on each man's take, but that didn't normally stop it. It was another problem Dudka had working with others, they got greedy.

Except tonight.

And, that's when Chuck knew they would kill him if they got the chance. Nobody else so much as mentioned money, which probably meant they had already come to an agreement. Most likely a three-way split—as soon as they had gotten rid of Chuck.

Tony Gregori mentioned he was hungry, and somebody else mentioned Barney's Deli was still open. Barney's was a dive, but they had great barbecue sauce—and there was a speakeasy on the corner, so whoever went could pick up some beer, too. Chuck volunteered, going so far as to write everybody's order on a notepad like a waiter, before he took off.

Then, strangely enough, he returned thirty minutes later.

He came back with sandwiches, side orders, and a dozen bottles of bootleg beer. The guys tore open the grocery bag and proceeded to lounge about a table and nearby couch, chowing down and talking about how great the sandwiches were—instead of business as usual. Chuck announced he was starving, then took his sandwich into a corner and began devouring it between sips of beer.

Less than five minutes later, Chuck looked up from his sandwich and smiled. All the other men in the room were frozen, their eyes wide, jaws hanging open as if locked, spittle crawling slowly from their mouths. Chuck watched them as he finished his own sandwich, then emerged from the shadows to take a closer look. Happy Malone's leg kicked in an effort to move, but it was impossible. His eyes begged for help.

"You guys feeling a little stiff or something?" Chuck laughed to himself, it broke into a musical sigh and then he announced, "The reason you can't move is because all your motor functions are paralyzed, even your reflexes. So far, it's the first symptom I've noticed in the use of cyanide poison. I'm guessing, though, that the hardest part for you guys is still coming. See, there's nothing you can do now except sit there, and watch me, watch you, die... And you'll still be watching, even after your heart's stopped beating, and you can't breathe—because I'm betting it's at least five minutes till your brain shuts down."

He turned toward Abandando, smiling.

"Not much of a loss in your case, huh Dasher?" Chuck put his sandwich down and walked over to observe the paralyzed Abandando. "Got to check out, you checking out," he muttered, repeating it to himself—visibly, pleasantly excited. He pressed one of the gangster's eyelids up further, gazing at his pupils. Then he struck a match on his shoe and waved it in front of the dying man's eyes, to see if there was any motor response to the light.

Chuck tossed his garbage, and the beer bottle with his fingerprints on it, into the same bag as the loot. Then he scoured the place for Abandando's possessions. After packing up some jewelry just waiting to be fenced, Chuck wiped down the rest of the room for prints and left.

On his way to the door he grabbed a beer for the road to celebrate. He'd not only just made thirty-thousand dollars, but he'd discovered a pretty good sandwich shop, too.

Still the consummate loner, Chuck eventually took an outside contract from another gang; then another, from a completely different gang. Word got around. Pretty soon Chuck Dudka was handling contract killings for at least four different mafia families—most of those involving one of New York's other crime families. Thanks to the *Cosa Nostra*, Chuck was making a killing. As the years passed, he continued to improve his skills with poisons, acids, knives, guns—even torture—and the highest bidder always found him.

New York 1937

Built around the same time Charles Dudka had been poisoning the Ocean Hill Gang, The Foley Square Courthouse stood like a monument to justice, just a few city blocks from the Brooklyn Bridge. Dead leaves swirled outside the building's entrance, until a tall, broad shouldered man strode through the lifeless autumn foliage. He snapped the brim of his fedora down to block the wind, and made his way beneath the ornate carvings of four ancient lawgivers—Plato, Aristotle, Demosthenes, and Moses.

Pulling an oversized hand out of his overcoat, the raw boned man scanned the interior of the building's white marble and noticed how similar the design was to the Supreme Court's. Then, he strode briskly toward an office in the rear, where the District Attorney's prosecutors were headquartered. Knocking twice to announce himself, he then opened the door.

Inside, three men sat behind an enormous wooden table covered with files and paperwork, fanned in arcing rows like fallen dominoes. Despite their groomed and tailored professionalism, the lawyers stared into the piles of paper as if trying to divine some higher meaning. A middle aged man with manicured fingernails and a conservative gray suit pulled a yellowed carbon copy out of one of the piles and stared at it a moment, before dropping it to glide across the table as he turned toward the man who had just entered the room.

In contrast to the men behind the table, the broad shouldered man's clothing didn't seem to fit quite right—yet, as he moved to close the door behind him and toss his fedora onto a coat hook, he moved with the grace of a gymnast or dancer. An ease of movement, as if rehearsed, that only began to hint at the man's complete muscular control. His face was more rugged than handsome, and still ruddy from the autumn wind.

"Inspector Dan Fowler, FBI," the young man said, introducing himself. His gunmetal, blue-gray eyes narrowed on the well-manicured attorney, accenting the collection of severe angles that formed the Inspector's face.

"Lawrence Keller, District Attorney," the man said, shaking Fowler's hand. "Glad you could make it, Inspector. With your testimony we may be able to tie Louis "Lepke" Buchalter to the Dutch Schultz hit in New Jersey. And if we can do that—we can finally take Frank Costello down." Costello, AKA "Frankie the Prime Minister" was the new and infamous leader of the Luciano Crime Family, who—along with his capos—now controlled organized crime from coast to coast.

"I appreciate your confidence," Fowler said, "but we both know the smoke from these gunmen rarely rises to the level of the boss giving orders."

"That's all right, Inspector. From what I've seen, your knowledge of the New York families trumps all the evidence we've gained from city *and* state officials. All we need you to do is to mark the points on organized crime's map. You just let us connect the dots. Judge Myers is sitting on the bench for this one, so odds of a conviction are on our side."

One of the younger attorneys seemed to stifle a laugh. Then said, "You know what Lucky Luciano's men call Myers?" to no one in particular.

"The Time Machine," Fowler said, a grin forcing the edges of his mouth up. "For the stiff sentences he hands out. Fats Brown was the first guy I ever heard say it. He was more worried about Judge Myers than being indicted."

"Well, we're fortunate to have Myers on the bench," the District Attorney said. "But that still doesn't guarantee a victory for the prosecution; we have to prove—without a doubt—Lepke's ties to Frank Costello and the rest of the syndicate." Keller glanced at his watch. "Court starts in ten minutes, men. Let's do this."

It was a short walk down the hall, where others on the D.A.'s staff already sat prepared at one of the tables before the judge. Behind the other table sat a high-priced syndicate attorney and Louis "Lepke" Buchalter, both of them with their hands resting on the table and whispering into each other's ears. The money spent on the two men's suits alone would have comfortably purchased a wardrobe for the entire District Attorney's staff.

Fowler sat down on one of the benches in back of the room, just in time to hear the bailiff announce:

"Ladies and Gentleman, the District Court for the Southern District of New York, docket number four-one-two-five, the honorable Judge William Myer's presiding, is now in session. All riiise!"

Fowler stood with the rest of the crowd, none of whom were actually related to anybody involved in the case but were, rather, a collection of reporters, students, curiosity seekers, and policemen. Most of the witnesses were sequestered in back, but one or two of their friends and relatives might have been there for support.

The judge, his jaw jutting out like the cowcatcher on a locomotive, stepped from behind a door in the corner and up onto the platform supporting the bench. He sat down and banged the gavel twice. Then, instantaneously, a puzzled look crossed his face, and a strange squeaking sound escaped from the back of his throat. The judges shoulder's hunched as if he were trying to push himself upright, and the gavel clattered to the floor. His face slammed down on the stained oak surface and slid, turning slowly, his robes trailing behind him to the floor.

Fowler remained where he was as the bailiff waved back the onlookers and crossed the courtroom to investigate. The newly promoted Inspector preferred his view from the back of the room, the better from which to deal with any criminal mischief likely to occur. However, since the defendant was out on bail, the whole concept of a breakout occurring would have been ludicrous. The ace FBI investigator was merely biding his time.

"Is there a doctor in the house?" The bailiff announced, popping up from behind the bench. The crowd muttered amongst themselves.

"I was a medic in the war," an older reporter said, as heads kept scanning the crowd. The newspaper man stuck his pencil in his coat and made his way up front. Fowler met him at the short, swinging doors that separated the court from the spectators. When they reached the judge's body, his eyes were already staring blankly into space, as if he were paralyzed or already dead.

The man from Associated Press checked for a pulse the same time as Fowler. There was none. The reporter attempted artificial respiration. While others stood enrapt by anxiety, knowing a life may stand in the balance, Fowler stood up and examined Judge Myers bench. His eyes rolled once over the top of it and on to the judge's seat, before he found what he was looking for.

With all the excitement, and the obvious lack of an assailant, it would have been easy to blame Judge Myer's condition on his health; already, the eyewitnesses were questioning whether he might have had a heart attack. But Fowler's quick eye soon proved the judge's condition had been triggered by a malignancy much less coincidental.

Attached to the bottom edge of the seat was a short, but inordinately wide, plunger type device, similar to a hypodermic syringe, but made of mostly of rubber. The tiny unit measured about the width of a silver dollar, and less than a half-inch deep. Fowler yanked it from its tape mounting, examined the mechanism and held it under his nose. A reporter behind the inspector yelped.

"You all right?" Inspector Fowler asked.

"Yeah, I just scratched myself on something in the judge's robe…" The reporter shook his head as if he were trying to clear it.

Fowler was standing beside the man in an instant, gently pressing Judge Myers' robes in between his hands, feeling up and down. "Aha!" he said, pulling something from the fabric. "Just what I thought, a small hypodermic needle." Fowler waved it under his nose like he was admiring a fine cigar.

The reporter looked up at the needle with a mixture of puzzlement, and then anxiety on his face. He seemed to be having trouble focusing his eyes. Sirens grew louder in the background.

"Did you call an ambulance?"

"Y-yeah," the reporter mumbled. "Don't think they can do anything. No heartbeat." Two medics stepped into the courtroom behind him.

"Medic! Over here! Forget the judge, I'm afraid it's too late," Fowler said, as they got closer. He grabbed the reporter by the shoulder. "This man scratched himself on the same needle that killed Judge Myers. I don't think he got a lethal dose, but he needs to be treated for poison immediately. Probably cyanide, but I'm guessing; there's an almond scent on the plunger."

Without a word, the two men placed the reporter on a stretcher and carried him out the door to the ambulance. Fowler continued to look down at the judge's lifeless body. Then he grabbed one of the District Attorney's men. "I need you to watch the body, make sure nobody touches it. This is a crime scene, now." He pointed at one of the D. A.'s other men. "You. I need you to grab the other bailiffs, all these cops, whoever you can find—make sure nobody leaves the courthouse. Now!"

The attorney made his way to the door, half the police followed him into the hallway. The two bailiffs stationed themselves on each side of the courtroom door. Nobody without a badge was getting out.

"Ladies and gentleman of the court! Inspector Fowler, FBI here! I need everybody to sit back down, or remain seated. This is a crime scene and we're going to need a list of witnesses." Fowler eyed the room, looking for anybody squeezing toward the door. Whoever the guilty party was, they weren't rushing to escape. In fact, given the nature of the murder weapon they probably weren't in the courtroom at all.

While the NYPD collected names and addresses, Fowler made his way to a row of phone booths in the lobby. "Inspector Fowler here, I need to speak with the director immediately."

Within minutes the case was Fowler's. With the FBI's New York office only blocks away, special agents Kendal and Harrison were en route to the courthouse within minutes. Fowler secured the crime scene while he waited, requesting a team of officers to keep watch on the door, and a portable crime lab, so he could dust for prints while he waited for the FBI's team to arrive.

A short time later, a stylish, dark-haired man in two-tone shoes entered the courthouse, trailed by a tall, blonde man with a dour expression on his face. The dark-haired man slung open the courtroom door and said, way too loudly: "I hear the New York Court System is murder this time of year!"

"Larry Kendal? What are you doing here?" Fowler stuck his head up from behind the bench where he'd been examining the judge's chair.

"Just finished working a case in Jersey," Agent Kendal said, "and The Chief suggested I might want to cross the river since these cockroaches all run in the same pack."

Brash, but always jovial, Larry Kendal was young for a Special Agent. Yet he had been with the FBI almost as long as Fowler, and had already proven himself countless times under fire. A bit of a clotheshorse, the tall, young man's fashion sense set him apart from others on the bureau as much as his quick thinking and bravery. Standing next to Dan he almost looked like a dandy, but as far as Fowler was concerned Larry's flash always transferred to whatever case he was working. Kendal pointed a thumb over his shoulder at the man behind him.

"Inspector Fowler, this is Agent Harrison, quite likely the most serious

"...his robes trailing behind him to the floor."

Irishman I've ever met—"

"Scotch-Irish," Harrison said.

"Quite likely the most serious Scotch-Irishman I've ever met," Kendal added without missing a beat.

"Nice to meet you, Agent Harrison. We could use a serious man. Right now we're in the middle of a gang war between Frank Costello and Salvatore Maranzano to see who takes over the Genovese Family, not to mention anybody else that may want to take over 'Lepke's' old gang."

"Word on the street is, there's a peace pact between the New York families; they've got some sort of crime commission now or something," Harrison said, his brow permanently wrinkled by his critical expression.

Fowler gave him a look like Agent Harrison had just tried to sell him the Brooklyn Bridge.

"Besides, we got five families in the city, and we know who heads each one of 'em," Harrison said. "So what family is Louis 'Lepke' Buchalter working for?"

"My guess," Fowler said, "is that there's some sort of mafia commission to keep the peace of that so-called pact, and that 'Lepke' works as some sort of enforcer for *all* the families."

"So, you think he put a hit out on the judge?" Kendal asked.

"It's possible. The obvious answer would be Costello or Maranzano arranged it, so 'Lepke' would get a lesser sentence than Judge Myers would hand out. But the problem is...even Costello's not that arrogant; it's too stupid a move. No, it's more likely somebody wants to frame Costello or Maranzano and get them out of the way.

"Agent Harrison, I want you to stay here, and make sure nobody contaminates the crime scene," Fowler continued. "Have a look around, you can dust for more prints if you want, but try not to touch anything. The boys in the 'flight squad' crime lab are already on their way. Larry, you and I will ask around the building, and see if we can come up with anything out of the ordinary. With any luck, we might just get a witness."

"Couldn't we just arrest Costello instead?" Kendal said.

"It's tempting." Fowler allowed himself the trace of a smile. He pulled off his hat and combed his hair back with the same hand, before setting it on back of his head. "But we both know we don't work that way."

"A man can dream can't he?" Kendal said, headed for the door. "Problem is, this thing is mobbed up with all five families. We're going to be running into a lot of brick walls—with very closed mouths."

"Then we'll have to knock 'em down, mouths included," Fowler said. "Remember, we're the only reason these animals act civilized. They may talk tough, but they're scared of us. Be cautious, but don't pull any punches, and don't stop."

"You don't have to tell me. I was in Chi for Capone." Harrison shook his head, tsk-tsking. "Two years. Two years of my life and the accountants got him," he said, exasperated.

"You did undercover?" Fowler said.

"Yeah."

"Pardon my asking," Agent Kendal said, with an amused expression on his face, "but were you trying to pass for Italian?"

"Armenian."

"And they still let you work on this side of the law?" Fowler teased.

"And here I was thinking he'd seen you, Dan—" Kendal barely concealed a wink. "—Saw the bureau was hiring the Irish, and figured they'd take anybody."

Both Fowler and Kendal looked as if they might laugh, but at most gave each other a nod before reaching into their coats for pen and paper. The two G-Men hit the hallway then headed separate directions on the stairs.

Questioning the janitorial crew, they learned that one of the maintenance men had failed to come in for work the day before. Two bailiffs gave descriptions of a tall, blonde haired man that had made that morning's rounds as janitor. Nobody else on staff even knew of the man. Working with the two witnesses, an FBI sketch artist rendered a rough portrait of the man. He was big, hadn't smiled, and the only time he had spoken, it had been with a soft, undetermined accent—possibly French, or Polish.

Fowler didn't know it yet, but it was a picture of Chuck Dudka.

Copies of the FBI artist's sketch were quickly plastered in the local papers and distributed among the NYPD, with every cop on the beat ordered to ask around. A search of the missing janitor's apartment revealed nothing. No one had seen him for days. The New York FBI office traced the backing of a rubber valve on the booby-trapped syringe to a Philadelphia manufacturer of plumbing supplies. Only two stores in the New York area carried the special valve, one of them in Brooklyn.

Agent Larry Kendal questioned the hardware store owner, who recognized the suspect in the bureau's sketch as one of his customers, but couldn't put a name to the face.

Then, a bartender at The Harp and Shamrock, a pub located only two blocks from the hardware store, called in to report that the man in the sketch was an occasional customer. When questioned, the bartender stated that the man had a thick Polish accent and rarely spoke to the regulars— but frequented meetings held in the back room, usually with some very rough looking characters. Kendal was seated at the bar within a half-hour, ordering bourbon and cokes in separate glasses, drinking the coke and pouring the bourbon on a potted plant that looked like it didn't have too long to live anyway.

While Agent Hamilton was stationed in the alley out back, Inspector Fowler kept his sharp features hidden behind a newspaper in a nondescript De Soto sedan across the street.

Sure enough, that same night, a big man with dirty-blonde hair and a two-hundred dollar suit walked through the front door of the Harp & Shamrock. Evidently his face had made the front page of one too many newspapers. The big man's mustache was missing, but he still fit the description. Kendal remained seated by the back door, trying not to draw attention to himself.

The big man ordered a beer and didn't drink it. Ten minutes later Anthony LaBragia, a local hood, came into the bar with another man. The man from the sketch flexed a nod toward a door next to the bar. The three men exited into the back room. Larry took his time until Dudka was out of view. Kendal made his way to the back door and waved to Harrison in the back alley, before ordering another drink and positioning himself on a stool by the front door. He'd been nursing his drink a good ten minutes, when the killer finally left the bar and rounded the corner headed west.

Fowler broadcast nothing on the police radio. He wanted to track the rat back to its nest, and he didn't want any interference from the local authorities. The G-Man started the car and pulled out ahead of the suspect, turning around the corner and parking ahead on the busy street. The man in the sketch walked right by him without even looking. Another man in a trench coat and two-tone shoes shuffled past about a minute later.

Larry Kendal had been born in the city. It was his element. He knew how to blend in with the background, even in two-tone shoes. He could tail a man through a metropolis as well as an Apache scout on the range. And, he could do it hiding out in the open, mingling with the crowd—blending in with the scenery when there wasn't any—hiding in plain sight. Kendal was never more than a block behind the burly suspect. The few times Dudka did turn around, the agent was either watching the killer's reflection in a storefront window, looking at his watch, or obscured by corner newsstands.

After wandering aimlessly for blocks, Dudka strolled to the door of a brownstone three-flat and went inside. Fowler pulled up across the street a half block away. Agent Harrison immediately stationed himself behind the house without a word. Kendal walked past the house, down the street and leaned in the De Soto's window.

"Radio for back-up yet?"

"Done. Problem is he's only a suspect. I'm waiting for public records information on the house."

Within minutes, the New York Bureau radioed in with the name of the owner, one Charles Stanislaus Dudka. There were no signs in the window to indicate he was renting out rooms, but, being a three-flat, entire floors could be occupied by innocent bystanders. Undercover cars pulled up discreetly around the four corners of the block. Fowler, and Kendal approached the door and knocked. Fowler's gun was already unholstered, in the pocket of his jacket.

The door opened a crack. Fowler held up his badge with the hand that wasn't gripping the .45 in his coat. "Mr. Charles Dudka? FBI. We'd just like you to ask you a few questions."

"FBI, eh? Uh, sure, no problem." With his accent the word "sure" sounded like "choor." The big man pushed the door open wider and stood there with a tin, pump spray can in one hand and a rag in the other. Without inviting the agents in, he turned his attention to polishing a mirror on the wall by the front door.

"So, Mr. Dudka, your description was given to us by witnesses of a crime and we have reason to believe your testimony might help bring that same criminal to justice," Fowler said, starting the questioning in as friendly a manner as possible.

"Choor," Dudka said, still polishing the mirror and dodging every question for the next six minutes. He insisted he had never witnessed a murder, he had never heard of Judge Myers, and he hadn't had a mustache for years—even though you could see the pale, razor-burned skin beneath his nose.

"One other thing, Mr. Dudka," Fowler said. "We traced part of a murder weapon to a hardware store in the neighborhood, and the owner, not to mention some other folks, identified you from this sketch."

Dudka's glare swung from the mirror to Fowler. "I'm doing a little remodeling on the house as you can see." He was grinning, but gritting his teeth, scowling down at the agent like he wanted to crush him. "And, I do a little contracting on the side..."

Fowler kept his cool. This was his man, he could feel it, but he had no way to prove it. He'd have to push him, stir things up. "Records show you were one of two people who purchased that particular plumbing valve—"

Dudka's eyebrows forced themselves together like he was trying to squeeze an eyeball out. Standing in the doorway, he shifted his feet and turned toward the two agents. Hairs on the back of Fowler's neck stood up.

"Don't breathe, Larry!" Fowler's left arm shot out, pushing Agent Kendal off one side of the porch, even as Dan launched himself off the other. Dudka's fist crushed the pump on the tin sprayer, and a light mist fired into the air where the agents had been a split-second before.

"There's something lethal in that glass cleaner!" Fowler said, as he hit the ground rolling and came up with his revolver in his hand.

Dudka was already gone. The two agents bounded through the door.

"I'll take upstairs," Larry said.

Fowler began to head for the kitchen, stopped, and with three strides tackled Agent Kendal at the bottom of the steps. A ratcheting sound, like some sort of giant trigger, clacked beneath their feet, and half the staircase exploded into shrapnel. Fowler was up before the sound had subsided.

"Larry, You OK?"

"I'm hit." Kendal lay back, his hands wrapped around a shin, blood leaking from between his fingers. "Go on! I'll keep an eye on the front door!"

Something in back of the house exploded. Fowler swung himself over the banister, and hit the ground running. Rounding the corner to the back door, he suddenly stopped. An almost invisible string-line extended across the path before him—a tripwire. He could also see a trail of thin fishing line waving in the autumn cool by the open back door. Agent Harrison lay on the porch, his hand over a hole in his gut, his eyes staring blankly at the sky.

"Don't move, Larry! This whole place is booby-trapped!"

At that same moment a New York Policeman, began to walk in the door. Fowler pointed his gun at him, forcing him to stop. "I'm Fowler, FBI. It's a trap. Call an ambulance, and then contact Agent Armbruster at the New York FBI Office; he's an explosives expert. Stay out, and keep the house surrounded."

Fowler grabbed Larry Kendal under the arm with his free hand, and helped him out the front door. Kendal's legs dragged behind him, leaving a trail of blood across the hardwood floor that smeared beneath his feet. Fowler left him on the porch. Two uniformed policemen pulled the wounded agent onto the lawn and began to administer first aid.

Back inside the house, Fowler picked up a bucket from the corner and placed it upside down over the pump can Dudka had dropped on the floor after spraying at them. The lab boys could analyze the contents later. Dan was willing to bet it was more cyanide.

Stepping vigilantly toward the kitchen Fowler spotted another thin string-line reflecting in the dim light from outside. Picking up a mop lying next to where the bucket had been, the inspector stationed himself around the corner. Using the wall for cover, he tripped the wire.

A panel attached to the string-line fell open. A gunshot fired, filling the air with smoke and buckshot, before a sawed off twelve-gauge was revealed. Had anybody simply walked into the kitchen, they'd be dead now. Fowler stepped to the middle of the room, mindful of every dust mote in the air as he slowly turned.

A minute later he spotted what he was looking for; one section of the kitchen floor tiles didn't match the others. An area of about a square foot was clean and the flooring unscratched—while all the other tiles surrounding it were dirty, scratched, some even yellowed. Fowler grabbed the frayed mop-handle, lay face down on the floor, and—using the splintered end of the handle as a lever—pried up a section of the flooring. It flipped up on a hinge, exposing a pit beneath it.

Pulling a pen-light out his shirt pocket, Dan shed some light on the subject, only to expose a series of stakes waiting to pierce the legs of anyone who lowered themselves inside unaware. Fowler spent about ten-minutes digging the stakes up with the mop handle. He dropped a washboard down on the floor to stand on and waited. Nothing happened.

He began to lower himself into the tunnel. Suddenly, before resting his foot on the floor, he stopped again. His eyebrows knitted together and both eyes circled the room suspiciously.

Fowler pulled himself back out. He picked a flour canister up off the counter and dropped it in the hole, expecting its weight to trigger another deadly trap. The canister hit the ground and a loud snap that echoed down the tunnel. The hairs on his neck were standing up again.

He stood straight, shining the flashlight into the hole for several minutes. Dudka had quite possibly already escaped, but if there was even the smallest chance of catching him the inspector knew he had to give chase. Dan lowered himself into the tunnel, gun in one hand, pen-light in the other. Shining the light ahead of him, he could see the path was narrow and meandering. He couldn't see five feet beyond the next curve, but continued to crawl on his hands and knees.

Rounding the first turn, he heard a rustling sound. Something small, moving in the dark ahead of him. *No, not something—*

A lot of somethings.

They were green, tiny, fast and fanged. Snakes, coming right at him.

Fowler had never seen one in real life, but he had seen pictures of them. Vipers, from the other side of the world—and they were every bit as poisonous, if not more so, than the cyanide the killer had used before.

Fowler fired his revolver, cutting the lead snake in half, then pulled the trigger until the gun was empty in hopes the sound might frighten the reptilian monsters. Adrenaline pumping, he slung his flashlight at the roiling nest of vipers and then turned, scrabbling back toward the trap door, kicking his feet behind him all the way. With no ladder rungs to pull himself up on, he planted hands and feet on opposite sides of the walls of the chute and scrambled upward, his limbs thrashing so hard he seemed to hang in the air a moment before his fingers clawed at the tile on the kitchen floor above him.

Yanking himself from the depths, Fowler spun on the floor and pulled his feet out. A viper gripped his right pant leg at the calf.

Fowler kicked his leg forward in a near-convulsive reflex, as if his muscles knew one glancing scratch meant paralysis and agonizing death. The venomous serpent's fangs tore free from his pant cuff, and the remaining force of the kick launched the reptile spinning through the air. The snake bounced off one of the floor cabinets, and the green demon's head shot upright, smoothly dancing from side to side, as if meditating on the best vein to strike.

Fowler feigned a step in its direction. The glistening killer hissed. Its head reared back for the strike, light sparkling off its fangs. Fowler picked up what was left of the mop handle and beat it to death. He pried the snake off the floor with the splintered tip of the handle, and looked at it dangling limply from the end—then threw it down and hit one more time, just to make sure, before he checked the calf of his leg to make sure he hadn't been bitten.

Straightening his jacket, Fowler stepped back out on the porch where he was greeted by policemen, a fire truck, and Agent Armbruster from the Bureau's New York office.

"This whole place is rigged," Dan said. "Nobody goes inside. It could take weeks to sift through." There was a brief pause as the men shuffled their feet impatiently. Fowler wiped his brow. "Somebody give me a shotgun."

Armbruster exchanged glances with another agent, and a Browning 12-guage pump appeared over Armbruster's shoulder butt first. Somebody else handed Fowler a handful of shotgun shells. The Inspector turned and went back into the building without another word.

Stepping just short of where Agent Kendal had been shot on the steps, Fowler fired two shots up the staircase. Another shot fired. Something exploded. Something else slammed. Dust from the falling plaster filled the upstairs.

Nobody outside had witnessed anyone fleeing the scene, which meant the mysterious assassin could still be here. Fowler headed down to the basement. He wasn't looking forward to dealing with another snake-pit. He fired a shot into the basement door. Nothing else exploded. The door creaked open on squeaky hinges. Just outside the door, Fowler could see the string that led to a single bare bulb in the ceiling. He fired the shotgun at it.

The stairs below pulled into themselves without a sound, exposing a series of sharpened bamboo stakes laid out in rows in front of him. Anyone not already dead, would have been crippled for life. Fowler gripped the doorjamb, leaned over and pulled the light switch. The bulb didn't illuminate much, but Fowler could see where three-inch wide steps remained next to the wall. Two steps down, he fired the gun into the path before him. Buckshot ricocheted, rattling around the room and bouncing off the brim of his hat.

At the bottom he could see the pull-chain of another bare bulb. While he could fire at the floor beneath him, the ace Inspector couldn't simply shoot into the darkness. He might not know who he was dealing with, but so far the sick-genius of this suspect suggested a blatant disregard for the value of human life—and the possibility of hostages.

He was reaching for the pull-chain when something hit him over the ear. Struggling to keep his balance, he turned to face his attacker. The blackness telescoped to a pinpoint of light. Then nothing.

Drifting in and out of consciousness, the fog in Fowler's head didn't clear as much as offer an occasional patch of awareness. He was paralyzed, curled up in a ball inside what was probably a large trunk. The fact that he could hear a motor and sense himself bouncing around meant the trunk was probably still belted to an automobile. He closed his eyes.

Eons later, bright light blinded him. The trunk fell off the back of the car and Fowler rolled out onto the dirt. He could hear Charles Dudka laughing behind him, but he couldn't turn his head to see. The contract killer had evidently unbelted the trunk and kicked it off the back of a Model-A. Fowler's eyes blurred. He didn't remember closing them.

After a minute or a week, something slapped him. At first he thought he was still in the gloom of the suspect's basement, until a shaft of light revealed a crag of moist rock in his peripheral vision. He didn't realize he'd felt a slap, until the same moment he became aware that he could turn his head to look around. A prickly feeling was returning to his legs, the paralysis was wearing off.

"You finally waking up, eh, G-Man?" The voice sounded like it was in a tunnel. Fowler didn't know how much of it was the cave he was in, or the state of his muddled brain.

The inspector tried to answer, but his mouth was taped closed. He tried moving his hands but couldn't. Spread eagled between four stakes in the floor, his hands and feet were bound by rope as if about to be drawn and quartered. Fowler turned his head in the other direction and looked directly into the eyes of the smiling assassin.

The big man struck a match and fired up a torch on the wall. When Dudka turned, the light revealed him positioning a camera mounted on a tripod. Some wiring ran from a wind-up alarm clock on the floor, up through the tripod and into the camera.

"Don't worry, G-Man. It's a camera, not a bomb," Dudka said, "More like… research. Besides, a bomb would be too easy for you. This is better."

Fowler tried to talk again. He wanted to ask why.

"You'll find out soon enough, G-Man. Y'know, it's funny, but you're probably the first guy I ever killed that wanted to ask a question. Usually they just beg. I hate that." He bent down, wound the alarm clock and said, "Y'see, sometimes I have clients that want something a little extra. They're willing to pay a little more, provided the target suffers some. Problem is, then I have to prove the target was still alive before the end. So I set this camera up to take a picture every few minutes." He checked the back of the

"Snakes coming right at him."

camera one last time before heading around a bend and into the light. "Be seeing you, G-Man. You won't see me."

Time passed. The torch on the wall went out, and the darkness closed in.

Fowler's head fell back into the dirt. He blinked the dust out of his eyes and tried to evaluate the situation. Looking up he could see the ceiling of the cave undulating. Then he heard the squeaking. Bats. But as threatening as the smell of guano was, Fowler couldn't see the danger. The bats grew louder, and eventually took off in a flock to hunt insects for the night. Even as his eyes adjusted better to the dark, there simply wasn't that much to see. The sun was fading around the bend in the tunnel. The darkness outside was rising to meet the darkness of the cave behind him.

Fowler's mind raced back to the snakes, but he tried not to think about that. Besides, he was outdoors, and he was pretty sure he was still in the states; those snakes were from Asia, and New York provided little in the way of jungle habitat. He scanned the walls for secret panels camouflaged to look like the side of the cave, but saw nothing. Dudka had already ruled out a bomb; he wanted his victim to suffer. Fowler thought about the wildlife upstate, bears, mountain lions. If this had been one of their dens Dudka would have been killed. But unless the walls opened up to reveal some sort of torture device, Fowler was willing to bet he was the bait for some wild animal. Maybe the snakes wouldn't have been so bad.

He closed his eyes and tried to collect himself. He was tired, sleepy, still feeling the effects of the drugs. Maybe if he fell asleep it would all be a dream, or at least he could rest until the end. "*No!*" a voice screamed from the veils of his subconscious. He couldn't fall asleep. Fowler flexed his arms and legs against his bonds one at a time. The stakes seemed to be part of the ground itself. Fowler gritted his teeth, and pulled with every fiber of his being. His head fell back to the ground as his limbs collapsed around him. Exhausted, his eyes closed and for a moment he thought he might have passed back out again.

Then he heard something. *Squeaking. The bats.*

It took him a minute to realize it was still too early for the bats to return. And, another minute to realize a difference in the pitch; it was more of a *screech* than a *squeak*. That same second, he sensed the slightest vibration, the pitter-patter of little feet. He glanced into the shadows above his head.

Rats. The cave was full of them.

They kept staring at him. Every few minutes, one of the vermin would separate from the pack and inch a little closer. When Fowler moved, they backed off, skittish.

They were still testing their meal. As long he could remain conscious and move, he might be safe—but as time passed the rats were becoming more and more impatient and, spurred on by the feast laid before them, ever hungrier.

Something nipped at his ear. *Damnit!* Fowler cursed himself and shook his head sending the rat back into the shadows. He must have passed out for a second. Even he knew he'd eventually reach the point of exhaustion. Till then, they'd keep nibbling him to death, piece by piece, until he could no longer scare them away. And the pack kept creeping forward, surrounding him until he moved, only to scurry back into the gloom once again.

The sun came up outside the cave. It went down again.

He was light headed, weak. His throat felt like a swollen wool blanket. Tired and thirsty, he was past the point of hunger. Dan Fowler's stamina was almost legendary within the bureau. He had easily worked cases some seventy-two hours without sleep in the past, but this time he had been drugged and fighting his bonds for more than twenty-four. Exhaustion had set in, he knew it, and the merest catnap would set off a feeding frenzy of ghastly proportions.

The camera on the tripod clicked, and the alarm clock attached to it started ticking. The timer had gone off and the camera was starting to take a picture every few minutes. Another sign it was mealtime.

Fowler could tell Dudka had emptied his pockets; even if he could reach them it wouldn't do any good. He rolled his head back and forth, forcing himself to stay conscious. His eyes closed. Something nipped at his ear, something else at his cheek. They were still just testing. When they had the opportunity, Fowler knew the first thing they would go for were his eyes. He set his teeth, the muscles of his jaw flexed. Then, the G-Man's steely eyes glinted with a fierce determination, before he did the completely unexpected. Dan Fowler closed his eyes; lay his head on the ground, and waited to be eaten.

The first nip came at his ear, just like before. This time Fowler didn't move. Tiny, sharp teeth sank in. Again, the only reaction was a flexing of his jaw as he felt the blood trickle down his neck.

The pack moved in closer. He could hear their footpads tapping the cave floor, their squeaks a sonic torture. Something bit his jaw. His mouth opened a little, a quiet gasp where any other man would have screamed. A slight, but unseen, shudder ran through his body.

Now the rats were nibbling at his calves and heels, the pack circled. He could feel them crawling on his chest. His eyes clenched shut, as he inhaled sharply. Still, he didn't move. Razor sharp teeth nipped at his jaw. Tiny claws climbed up his neck. Something with matted fur skittered up the edge of his mouth and nipped at his eyelid. It was what Fowler had been waiting for.

Dan's head snapped into the air like a crocodile exploding from the depths. His teeth gripped the rat in his mouth. As the rat pack swirled back into the shadows, Fowler's jaw clenched again. He could hear the bones break, and blood ran warm across his tongue.

There was a moment of silence. Fowler coughed, gagging, but held the rat in his mouth. His left hand dug into the cave floor, scraping a small pit in the dirt, just big enough to hold his hand. He pulled the rope to the floor, testing his hand position. Then, he held his left hand as high in the air as possible, still gritting his teeth around the rat, his lips spread wide. Fowler inhaled and exhaled like a weightlifter about to jerk, and almost gagged again. Then, he inhaled sharply, turned his face to the right, and slung his head—hard, back to the left—flinging the rat's black corpse into the air.

In Fowler's fatigued, near unconscious state it seemed to hang there. Time stopped.

Thup, the tiny corpse hit the cave floor. With a sudden rush of adrenaline, Fowler slammed his hand into the divot he'd dug in the ground, and the rope pulled taut on top of the tiny pile of bone, fur, and blood. The sea of vermin roiled and flowed around the captive corpse of their fellow rat, like a single organism drilling for the jugular.

Fowler kicked his right side and the furry blanket backed away, only to poke and prod back into the daylight, testing as if it might set them on fire. The Inspector inhaled, exhaled, controlling his breathing to avoid panic. Then, he lay still, and waited another eternity.

Anything moving to his right, Fowler kicked and twisted to keep away; it wasn't too hard, they were still skittish. But his left arm, no matter what, could not move. He had already figured he might lose his hand on a gambit like this.

Still, the camera clicked again.

A pair of bright eyes appeared in his peripheral vision. Fowler didn't turn to meet them. "Come on, baby… C'mon…" he whispered under his breath. Spurred on by the taunting feast laid before him, the tiny monster began tearing at the corpse of its brother. Fowler ground the rope into the corpse of the rat that had been in his mouth only moments before, and two more sets of eyes signaled from the dark, coming forward to nibble. A wave of fur enveloped them as the pack stampeded, roiling in a feeding frenzy. Fowler shut his eyes, his left arm keeping the rope taut, the only thing in his mind.

Finally, something gave. His hand clenched higher in the air—only a half-foot or so, but that was a mile compared to only seconds ago. Quickly, he slammed his hand back into the ground. The pack was so ravenous they didn't even notice. Fowler waited until he could stand it no more, then jerked his hand—high and hard—to the right. Only one strand of braided rope remained. Fowler yanked again, the last of his strength. His hand shot to his belt buckle.

The rats were still all over him, like a wave of teeth and fur. Even shaking and slamming himself on the ground wouldn't keep them off anymore. The G-Man's belt popped from his hip like a bullwhip—the buckle lashing vermin off his legs in a swathe. Then the leather blurred around him, its silver clasp a bulleting dervish. The pack scurried for cover where the rocks met the shadows.

Exhausted and with no concept of time, the ten minutes it took Fowler to untie himself seemed like forever. He stumbled to his feet, suddenly aware of the daylight outside. Bracing himself against the wall, he stared back into the darkness, for the first time aware of what had been behind him. A pit. Dark and dank, it sat in the cave's rear wall, surrounded by scattered bones already picked clean.

Fowler suspected this was where the body of the unfortunate courthouse janitor Dudka had impersonated probably wound up. Dan stumbled toward the camera and grappled the tripod in one arm, so he could look at the evidence in the daylight. Then his foot slid on something, and he nearly tripped.

It was the matchbook Dudka had used to light the torch. On it was the name of an Italian restaurant: Dagastino's. And—like that— Fowler's fatigue evaporated; he was working on a case.

Clearing the cave entrance, Fowler judged from the sun it was morning. He pulled a staff-sized walking stick from the leaf encrusted forest floor, and headed down a dirt road that was little more than a trail with the camera in his hand. Two miles down the road he spotted a farmhouse and knocked on the door. The farmer didn't have a phone but, after his wife cleaned and bandaged Fowler's wounds, he was more than willing to drive the G-Man into the nearest town. Fowler called the Bureau's New York office for a car, then sat in a rocking chair on the porch of the dry-goods store, waiting.

When the car arrived, Larry Kendal was in the passenger seat sporting a cane. He pointed at the driver by way of introduction.

"Inspector Fowler, Agent Cassaday from the New York office."

Fowler appeared to barely glance up, until the driver turned to wave hello. Dan's frozen stare melted as he took in the new agent's face. The man was almost a double for Agent Harrison, could have been his little brother. Fowler had forgotten about the death of Agent Harrison, or at least managed to wipe it from his memory—until he faced this new, younger, yet-to-be-doomed version of the agent whose life had ended only hours ago on Dan's watch.

Agent Kendal raised an eyebrow and one side of his mouth in a knowing half-smile over Cassaday's shoulder, as if to say "Ain't life crazy." Before Larry could mention they had brought a change of clothes for Dan, Fowler sat down and slammed the car's rear door.

"Coney Island, boys—and step on it," the inspector sighed.

"Coney Island?" Kendal said, flexing his weight on the cane's handle to peer into the back seat. "Look, Dan, I think the lines in that place are as criminal as anybody, but... We're going to roust Coney Island?"

"No, Larry. We're going to roust the mob."

"Well, take that, tilt-a-whirl," Kendal answered, punching the air. He still had no idea what they were going to do.

Rounding the bridge to Coney Island, Fowler finally told his fellow agents their destination. Dagastino's restaurant, a tiny Italian eatery on the edge of Coney. It was also a headquarters of sorts for certain lieutenants of the Bonanno crime family. Agent Cassaday waited in the car. Larry was just happy there wasn't a line to get inside.

Seated at a table in back of the restaurant was a thin man eating from a plate of spaghetti the size of his head. His dark hair was slicked straight back, his double-breasted suit obscured by a checkered napkin tucked into his collar to ward off the tomato sauce.

The man's name was Gilbert Gianni. He was rumored to be one of Joey Bonanno's lieutenant's, and word on the street was Bonanno was about to leave the country. That left three different underbosses to run the organization. Not the best of odds, even for a "made" man. Gianni barely looked up from his plate except to retrieve his wine glass. That's when he looked up at Fowler.

The two men recognized each other at first sight. Dan stood across the table from the mobster, both fists resting on the tabletop. Two of Gianni's bodyguards glared at Fowler with eyes like knives, until Larry Kendal pulled a chair from the table with the handle of his cane, sat down before them, leaned back and smiled. The two torpedoes backed away when Gianni, forced to turn his attention from his meal, stared them down with the tiny black slits he called eyes.

Fowler remained standing. "Where's Charles Dudka?"

"Waitaminnit, G-Man. Dudka? You mean that Polish killer? Even if I was involved in this organized crime outfit you speak of—which I'm not," Gianni said, in a voice trained to hide all but the wisp of an Italian accent, "—but even if I was, you should know by now, I am not a rat."

"I didn't hear anybody mention organized crime, but you," Larry said, grabbing a breadstick from the centerpiece.

"He honestly thinks this is organized, Larry," Fowler said, leaning over the table, and staring into the gangster's eyes. "But I'm here to tell you, you've got a rogue killer out there, Gianni. If he hasn't slipped through the roadblocks they put up—then he's a danger to you. Because this man will take a contract from anybody, on anybody. And, considering there are three of you jockeying for 'Joey Bananas' job, it's highly likely somebody's going to want you out of the way."

"I can take care of myself, Fowler," Gianni said, his accent becoming more prominent with anger. He fidgeted with his fork, before clenching it in his hand like a dagger and stabbing at his spaghetti again. "An' like I said—even if I did know somethin'—I wouldn't know nothin'! I'm an upstanding citizen, G-Man!"

"You like this cream sauce?" Larry asked, poking his breadstick into the the edge of Gianni's plate.

The gangster looked at Larry like was from outer space.

"Because something like this—" Larry sniffed the breadstick "—would be really easy to slip some kinda' poison into, y'know? Dudka likes cyanide, and—in this case—I think I'd have to agree with him. You notice a sort of nutty flavor in there? You probably wouldn't, until it was too late."

Gianni opened his mouth to say something. Fowler interrupted.

"Assassin like that, he's not going to poison a whole restaurant, Larry. Gianni knows that. Heck, I'm willing to bet he hasn't left here for days. He thinks we're going to catch his contract killer for him, but he's missing the big point: Dudka likes killing, and he likes to build traps—the more time he has out on the street, the more time he's got to build his little traps. We wouldn't be here if we had a clue to his whereabouts, Gianni, and if it takes us another week to find Dudka, that's seven more days he's got to booby-trap *everything you own, and everywhere you go.*"

"How long do you think it would take him to slip something into your toothpaste or your hair oil, Gianni? Bombs in your cars, boats, homes, hideaways. Gas, bullets, knives, poison—heck, even animals! This guy does love his work," Larry added.

Gianni shot a glance at his henchmen. They stood up and left.

"OK, G-Man, now we can talk. I simply can not have uncertainties spread among my…" Gianni lapsed.

"Organization?" Larry finished.

"Investors." The gangster smiled, then turned and pointed at Dan with his fork. "But you—you make sense, Fowler. Not that I'm scared, it's just that this kind of thing is bad for business."

"Dying usually is."

Gianni began writing out a list. Obviously, the gangster wasn't willing to expose any of his own crimes, and none of the names he gave would be part of his organization; the bureau would still have their work cut out for them. Gianni smiled and handed Fowler the list.

Larry shot Dan a sidewise look across the table like they were reading each other's mind. *It was too easy.*

"You know something just struck me funny, Gianni. I thought you were supposed to be one of those tough guys…but you just folded like an accordion."

"Oh, I'm tough enough, Fowler. And, I am not a criminal," Gianni muttered.

"Not a very good one," Larry said, and the two G-Men headed for the door.

"No, not good at all," Fowler whispered back, once they were outside. "He's in on it. He's not scared, because Dudka's working for *him*."

"Gianni was trying frame up Maranzano?"

"Or Frank Costello—"

"—who's a hell of a lot scarier than Dudka!"

"Larry, I want you and Cassaday to drive around the block and phone in for back up. When you get back, stay out of sight and keep your eye on the front door. I'm going around back."

The instant the front door had stopped swinging behind the two FBI agents, Gilbert Gianni had torn the napkin from his collar, jumped from his chair and strode briskly toward the kitchen service door. Cursing under his breath as cooks and servers stepped out of his way, the angry mobster tore open the door of a broom closet. Then he tore open a hidden door in back of it, revealing shadowy concrete stairs leading into the darkness. A secret, basement room. Gianni leaned into the darkness and pulled a chain, igniting a single bulb.

"Coast is clear Dudka! You gotta move though! Now!"

The torpedo's face appeared out of the shadows, the razor burned skin beneath his nose like a frown. "But—but where will I go?"

"I dunno, but it's too hot here! Feds are questioning everybody! Look, here's some money." Gianni shoved a wad of bills into Dudka's hand. "Find a fleabag hotel till things cool down. They can't keep the whole city cordoned off forever. Then you can scram."

Dudka nodded, dumbly. "You—you kicking me out?"

"Look around, ya dumb Polack. This is a restaurant. Ya can't spend the rest of your life in the broom closet! Get a room, get a girl, get a couple o' bottles. By the time you sober up this'll all be over."

"But…" Dudka looked like the same lonely kid he'd been ten years before, as if he were hiding from the same bully tormenters all over again.

Gianni grabbed the assassin by his wrist and started shoving him toward the back alley exit. The two men made eye contact.

"Waitaminute, Dudka, you're not scared are ya?" He chuckled, almost to himself, suddenly stopped and said, "Guy like you's got no reason to be afraid."

Dudka's hand flew for his coat. A .45 automatic fired twice, point blank, at Gianni's chest. The restaurant owner's body fell face down on the steps and thumped its way down into the darkness. Gilbert Gianni would never laugh at Charles Dudka again.

"The two men recognized each other..."

The assassin strolled to the restaurant's rear exit, gun still in hand. Clearing the door, the light framed his silhouette, and the crack of a warning shot echoed off tenement brick.

"FBI, Dudka! Drop the gun!" a voice roared from the shadows.

Dudka's profile stiffened when he heard the voice of his supposedly dead victim. The contract killer fired into the darkness and turned to run the other direction.

A shot rang out. The bullet peeled across Dudka's back and chopped at his rib cage. The contract killer's hand clutched at his side as he bounced off a wall going around the corner. Fowler was hot on his trail.

Dodging through traffic on 15th street, Dudka managed to hop a trolley car and snake his way down Surf Avenue, before hopping off again. Before he had a chance to round the next corner, the trolley pulled away like a stage curtain revealing Fowler on the sidewalk across the street, his gun at his side, eyes staring directly into the contract killer's.

That damned G-Man! Dudka's jaw dropped with his hopes. Still clenching his side, he scuttled for the next intersection, pushing through the afternoon crowd.

A black sedan bumped up on the sidewalk in front of him. Agent Larry Kendal sat on the car's passenger windowsill, aiming a Thompson sub-machinegun at him over the car.

A squeaking, panicked sound leaked from the killer's throat. He turned back around, fired at Fowler through the afternoon crowd and charged. Dan stood in firing position, arms extended, waiting for a shot that didn't endanger the late afternoon crowd. He never got it.

Dudka seized a woman's handbag, slung the screaming female at the G-Man and ran back into traffic. Tires screeched as swerving cars dodged and scraped in the middle of the street. Dudka yanked the driver out of a Pierce Arrow by the collar. The man took a swing at him and the killer shot him in the stomach. Before the body had dropped in the street, Dudka leapt behind the wheel of the car and floored the accelerator, away from the intersection. Agent Cassaday wheeled the bureau's car up on the sidewalk and around the wreckage, then pitched it back onto the street in pursuit. Fowler jumped on the running board as the bureau car passed and held on tight.

Dudka could drive. Like an expert. The Pierce Arrow was not a small car, and yet the big man steered around traffic, swerving in and out of lanes, around corners, and through intersections on a dime. Vehicles crashed around him, not one touched the getaway car.

Agent Cassaday was a driver, too. While the Bureau's sedan was heavier, it was not one of their bulletproof armored cars and so easier to maneuver. But Cassaday used the car's weight in the turns, pinwheeling around corners like a professional dirt track driver. Fowler's iron grip clasped him to the car door with one hand, while the other arm stood extended, his finger tightening on the trigger of his service revolver. Two shots fired, and one of the Pierce Arrow's rear tires exploded, flinging shreds of spinning rubber into the air.

The getaway car veered hard right, taking out a corner newsstand and narrowly missing the vendor inside. Agent Cassaday slung the bureau car at an angle in front of it, even as Dudka crawled from the other side of the wreckage, backtracking and using the newsstand's remaining corner for cover.

The assassin wiped the blood out of his eyes from where his face had hit the windshield and used the distraction of the accident to make way for the nearest alley. Rounding the corner, he looked back to see Fowler and Agent Kendal making their way around the wreckage, guns drawn, still covering the newsstand.

At the alley's exit he stopped to lean against the wall, and reload. Pulling his hand from his ribs, he noticed all the blood for the first time, as he popped a fresh clip in the automatic. Shoving himself away from the support of the wall, he staggered and stopped. They were right behind him. He had to hide.

Soon, the footsteps of justice echoed down that selfsame alley, and a long shadow cast itself on the bricks where Dudka had rested only moments before. A hawk-like gaze detected the drops of blood on the ground where the assassin had stopped. As he turned toward the alley's exit, something hit the G-Man in the head. His vision narrowed to a white dot. His hands extended, trying to balance, and he sank to his knees. A hand like a mallet reached in his coat. A gun cocked by his ear.

Dudka had been hiding in the garbage—a stack of crates, ashcans, and detritus.

"You're coming with me G-Man."

A hand lifted him in the air by his hair. A gun poked at his ribs. The G-Man swayed unsteadily but did not collapse. Dudka pushed his near-unconscious hostage away from the street, down the intersecting back alley, and in the back door of an abandoned warehouse garage. The same warehouse Dasher Abandando's gang had died in five years before.

Dudka slammed the G-Man into a corner, and hit him over the head again. Pulling a sawed off shotgun from under a corroded workbench, the killer wrapped a length of wire around the gun's barrel, then tied it around the agent's neck, so the barrel was wedged directly at the base of the investigator's skull. One false move, one tug, and the victim would pull the trigger himself.

Struggle and he'd blow his own head off.

"Where's Agent Cassaday?" Inspector Fowler asked.

Both Fowler and Agent Kendal had launched themselves from the car the moment Cassaday had pulled up in front of the newsstand. After circling the wreckage, Agent Kendal had run to a drugstore and called in an emergency, while Dan administered first aid to the newsstand's owner.

Kendal glanced back at the Bureau's sedan. "I thought he was with you."

"Find him. Something's not right here." Fowler's head turned, scanning the area. Agent Kendal was already heading to the opposite side of the intersection, when Dan's eye's stopped on the alley entrance across from the front of the wrecked car.

Soon, another shadow fell across the blood puddled in the alley, except this one wore the snap brim fedora of The Civilian Gladiator. Fowler nudged the blood with his toe, to see if it had had any time to dry. It was still wet, just a little darker around the edges. Whoever had been here was badly wounded. The inspector noted the scrapes around the ash cans and the pebbles on the ground, pointing their way like an arrow to the next blood spatter where two alleys intersected. The back alley was newly paved, not a print or a drop on it. Fowler made his way down it and around the block. Nothing.

Stopping at the corner, Dan glanced down the street at something almost familiar. There, in the middle of the block, was an auto garage. He pulled the list of cold leads Gianni had given him back at the restaurant from his pocket.

Gianni's list had included only three locations in Brooklyn. The first, an abandoned bar and grill, was already opening under a new owner. The second, a mob-owned, machine shop the locals still called "the Tool and Die"—Fowler had already marked off the list as too conspicuous. But the third…

The third location was a warehouse garage, right here at the end of Stillwell Ave, where four mobsters had been found poisoned some eight years ago, their sandwiches laced with cyanide. The case was still unsolved.

Fowler circled around the back alley and tried the garage's rear door. It was unlocked. The inspector nudged the door open, and peered into the scattered shadows within. Judging from the blankets and food wrappings somebody had been hiding out here. He stepped briskly through the office and into the warehouse.

"Drop it, G-Man." Dudka took a step out of the darkness, dragging Cassaday across the concrete by the shotgun wired around the agent's neck. The killer glared at Fowler from behind the .45 automatic's sights.

Dan opened his hand. His service revolver clattered to the floor. Cassaday might have coughed; it was hard to tell if he was still alive, or if Agent Harrison's double was about to be murdered all over again. Dudka's finger tightened on the trigger.

Fowler needed a distraction, anything. He kicked his gun across the floor toward the contract killer. Dudka's eyes followed the gun.

Fowler's gaze scoured the corners, his vision still adjusting to the darkness. "You can shoot me, but it won't do you any good—the cavalry's on its way. Once Costello finds out about Gianni's frame-up, you're both as good as dead. It's just a matter of who kills you."

Dudka stared at him blankly. Before, Fowler had looked into the killer's eyes and seen nothing. No hope, no fear, no love. Nothing but the emotionless, black-button stare of a shark. This time, though, something was different. This time, there was just the tiniest glimmer of something. Hate may have ruled the center of the contract killer's stare, but the tiniest glimmer of something else was wriggling in around the edges.

Fear.

Dudka wiped the blood from his face. His gaze shifted—side to side— then over his shoulder, looking for a way out.

Something gleamed in the periphery of Fowler's vision. Something metal. A weapon. Fowler didn't know it, but it was Happy Malone's old meat cleaver, the one that had impressed the young Charles Dudka so many years before. The same razor-sharp cleaver that had terrorized the south side all those years ago sat gathering dust on the shelf like an artifact in some abandoned attic. Fowler kicked at the ground again, like he was scooting another gun across the floor. The killer's eye moved to follow it.

The G-Man's left hand shot behind him into the dark. Dudka's arm flexed, ready to fire—and a silver blade spun through the scattered light like a demon spark in hell.

Dudka saw a flash. Something hit him in the left arm, and his hand went numb. A second gun clattered off the floor. Then, something else hit him in the side of the head. Dudka thrashed his arms blindly and hit something, then loped for the side exit, dragging Agent Cassaday behind him.

The contract killer's blow had dazed Fowler, and Dan had been forced to kneel a moment, battling for consciousness. Every bite, bruise, cut, and minute without sleep was taking its toll. Feeling his way across the floor, Dan found his revolver, and slid back into standing position. Then, as if possessed, he strode slowly out the door and onto the boardwalk.

Coney Island Amusement Park was almost abandoned this time of year, not quite closed for winter, but practically vacant except for the occasional booths where sideshow freaks and fortune tellers lived until carnival season. The Observation Tower stood stark and cold in the distance like a monument at a cemetery watching over the gravestones. The Cyclone Rollercoaster twisted in the background, a decaying serpent held at bay by the frozen Wonderwheel.

Dudka had both hands on the shotgun now, his weight pressing against the sawed-off so hard, it was tough to tell if he was shoving it into Cassaday's head or using it to keep himself upright. He wiped his bloody brow and stared ahead in a fog.

"What are you going to do, Dudka, bleed on him?" Fowler's gun hung at his side. "Look at yourself."

Dudka eyes looked as if they connected to his brain for a second. He glanced at one arm, then the other. His whole left side was covered with blood. It ran down his arm in a stream where the cleaver had chopped him. He looked back up and his eyes focused on Fowler.

"You're losing too much blood. Another pint, you won't be able to stand up," the G-Man reasoned. "You're already dead."

The corners of the assassin's mouth turned up, and he leaned on the shotgun. Blood frothed from the corner of his mouth as he spoke. "It's got a… hair trigger."

Fowler's arm jerked erect as if mechanically sprung. A hole appeared between Dudka's eyes and something blew out of the back of his head.

The gunshot echoed hollowly in the salt air. The killer never heard it.

Dudka collapsed sideways as if pulled by the sea. Dry, empty, sea shells cracked beneath someone's feet in the background. Agent Kendal. Fowler waved him forward then collapsed to his knees.

Kendal checked Agent Cassaday's pulse first, then untied the shotgun from his neck. Cassaday's eyelids fluttered, and a few minutes later he was stumbling around on his feet.

Fowler sat up, and Larry pushed him back down with the heel of his palm. He held one of Dan's eyes open with his thumb, checking for signs of shock. "You alright?"

"Yeah, I think so." Fowler stared up at the gunmetal sky, watching the seagulls circle silently above. A siren echoed in the distance. Two gulls landed on the beach behind them, then two more.

Larry pulled Dan to his feet, and soon all three of the G-Men were forcing their wounded way toward the boardwalk. With Cassaday at risk for concussion, and Agent Kendal still walking on a cane, the three men had to stop and rest on a park bench. They sat down and stared out at the beach, waiting for the police and watching, as the sea-birds began feasting on the predator's corpse.

The End

Feeding on the Predator's Corpse

OK, I admit it. Charles Dudka is Richard Kuklinski.

See, every good hero needs a good villain, so once in a while I'll read a little true crime. And if you don't know who Richard Kuklinski is, then by all rights you probably sleep a little better at night than the rest of us.

Nicknamed "The Iceman" because he'd once frozen one of his victims and then left him to thaw to confuse investigators, Kuklinski was a real-life hitman from the Bronx—a bona fide sociopath who claimed to have ended over two-hundred-and-fifty human lives. And, while I might have changed a lot of the details, his story parallels that of Charles Dudka quite closely at the beginning.

Kuklinski's first kill was a neighborhood bully he stuffed into the trunk of a stolen car and buried in the woods upstate. And, just like in the story, the only thing that bothered him was that it didn't bother him. In his late teens and early twenties Kuklinski would go to the bowery in the late night/ early morning hours and practice his deadly craft on panhandlers and street people. I can only begin to imagine how he would have eviscerated today's more aggressive and mentally ill panhandlers and homeless.

Like Dudka, Kuklinski had no problems killing police, judges, mobsters, or union officials. He liked the bodies to look like an accident or disappear completely. And, if the big boys were willing to pay a little extra, he would feed live victims to the rats, setting up an automatic camera beforehand to film their grisly work. While his employers were quite often delighted by the results, many of them were appalled at the same time. So, not only did other sociopaths consider The Iceman sick, but they were scared of him. That's right, Kuklinski was the one guy even the mob bosses were frightened of.

The poisoning scene in the garage remains very close to the truth. And, as someone that's seen the results of poisoning on animals in the wild, I can only say I still find it terrifying. In fact, one of the only things scarier is that once this monster discovered he could mix cyanide with water, and spray an election official in the face on a windless day, it became his favorite method of killing. Many of his victims weren't autopsied until years later and it was assumed had died of heart attacks.

Yup, ol' Richard liked to watch his victims die, slowly, and the one thing that held more interest for him than anything was that moment as he watched the last vestiges of life drain from his victim's eyes.

You may think having one hitman who worked for all five of the New York mafia families would have to be a work of fiction; it's not. Bottom line, with all those mobsters fighting for a seat at the top of the heap of skulls, it was convenient to have somebody like The Iceman around.

In real life it was Kuklinski's love of cyanide that eventually got him caught. Since cyanide was regulated and it sources were few (usually veterinarians), the FBI set up a sting. Already surprised by the information they had on The Iceman, as years went by and the entire story was revealed, the truth turned out to be even more shocking.

So I had the perfect villain for the world's greatest G-Man.

Now come the apologies.

For the purpose of my story I had to make the character an immigrant, and since Kuklinski was of Polish descent I decided to leave him that way; it is in no way a denigration of Polish-Americans, nor is it the punchline for a lousy joke. In fact, I've worked construction with a hell of a lot of Polish immigrants, and while we didn't even speak the same language, I always found them to be superior craftsmen and wonderful people. Hell, I live in Chicago, and they probably built half the adopted hometown I continue to harbor a love-hate relationship with. Remember, as far as I'm concerned everybody in the world is a seventh-cousin and we need to learn to get along.

Now, having decided that the villain would be Polish-American, I needed a name. For me character's names are best when real, and still say something about the character—so I didn't want to use the stereotypical ones like Cowsnofski or Pulaski.

Enter the Dudka family—the real ones, not the fictional.

See, my wife and I buy, sell, and trade a lot of vintage goods, and I have to admit it's pretty cool way for a lowly pulp scribe like myself to earn a few extra bucks while surrounding himself with many of the elements of his stories. While sampling the wares of an estate sale in Indiana, we were lucky enough to have met part of the Dudka family tree. I mentioned my need for a Polish moniker that wasn't stereotypical, and one of them offered up their mother's maiden name. There was no way I couldn't use it. Dudka—like "dead kill." It was perfect, although I'm not really sure the family knew my villain might make their mom spin in her grave.

So, apologies offered. And, if it helps any I'll remind you that Mary Bell, my family's namesake, was one of the scariest child murderers ever offered the European press. She liked to watch people die, too—except in her case they were other children.

Most of the Fowler stories I've read start with an incident, and then The Chief calls Dan into his office, but I figured since the action was all going to be centered in New York I could get to it faster if I set up Dan to testify at a trial. The poison syringe on the judge's bench is my own invention. I don't think one would be too hard to make, and it seemed like an even faster way to get Dan in on the action. Then, once I had it set up, all I had to do was let Dan, Larry and the rest of the gang do their job, which made mine that much easier.

I tried to keep the information regarding the Mafia's five families as historically accurate to 1937 as possible, but all the Italian characters actually appearing in the story were made up. And, while this isn't exactly historical fiction, I think I did a pretty good job.

I did put the Dudka character in Brooklyn instead of the Bronx, because I knew I wanted to end the story on Coney Island, and, I couldn't resist the temptation to make my murderer from the Gravesend neighborhood. C'mon, a killer from Gravesend? How could I not?

As always, I'd like to offer my thanks to Ron Fortier, Rob Davis of Airship 27 Productions for once again allowing to me to be a 21st Century pulp writer. And the hits just keep on a-coming!

And while we're at it, in case you're curious, the hardest part of any so-called "research" for this story came from my own past. I once spent a weekend bleeding internally in Madison, Wisconsin, and was surprised to discover that the average male only has about twelve pints of blood; women, about ten.

But I'm feeling much better now.

In part, thanks to you, dear reader. I hope you enjoyed it.

BYRON CHRSTOPHER BELL - is the author and creator of *Tales of The Bagman*, Chicago's very own pulp hero. He has also written Airship 27 Adventures for *Secret Agent X, Jim Anthony: Super-Detective*, and the first volume of *Dan Fowler G-Man* adventures. An award winning short-story writer, Bell is currently working on a tribute to Black Mask Magazine pulp writer Paul Cain's novel *Fast One*, and a World's Fair sequel featuring Mac McCullough, The Bagman. He is lucky to live with his wife in "the city where the weak are killed and eaten."

Join him on Facebook, or at his weblog: http//chicagobagman.blogspot.com

The Long Haul

Oftentimes readers believe a book like this one just comes together in a few months. They see us recruiting writers, artists, cover painters, assembling everything into a nice pulp package and getting it off to the printers with nary a hiccup.

Nothing could be further from the truth. The book you have just finished reading, and hopefully enjoyed, is nearly two years old now. The truth is that in any endeavor dealing with brilliantly creative individuals there are always going to be detours and hazards totally unforeseen at the beginning of the project. This is one of the main reasons we at Airship 27 Productions never set deadlines for any of titles.

When DAN FOWLER G-MAN Vol I was released, it was very well received by both critics and fans. Fowler is such a well known and loved classic pulp character; we weren't surprised his first new adventures in decades went over extremely well and so were eager to put together another book. We put out the word through our regular channels and almost immediately had filled out a roster with four of the best New Pulp writers in the business; Derrick Ferguson, Aaron Smith, Josh Reynolds and B.C. Bell. All of these fellows had worked with us before and we knew their tales would not only be great, which they are, but also be submitted in a timely fashion.

The real challenge was finding the appropriate art team to embellish this new volume both with a dynamic new cover painting and some exciting interior illustrations. Whereas Brian McCulloch had done a gorgeous Sherlock Holmes cover for us (volume III) we turned to him as our choice for cover painter and were thrilled when he happily signed on. We had only one final element to our book puzzle mission, someone to draw the interior pieces, three for each tale.

I've a habit of trolling internet sites where graphic artists congregate and it was at one of these that I happily discovered sample art by Neil Foster. I was instantly impressed with his command of composition, anatomy and skills with both penciling and inking. If he could capture the styling of the era, then I was convinced he was the artist for this job. I approached Neil, explained our operations here at Airship 27 Productions and invited him to join the project and was rewarded by his enthusiastic yes. So our team was assembled and it was time to get cracking on DAN FOWLER G-MAN Vol II.

Within six months several stories had come in, Brian had begun preliminary work on this cover composition and Neil had turned in a few spot illos for the first story. Everything read and looked fantastic. It was all too clear to this editor and that we had another winner on our hands.

Then tragedy struck and everything went south in a heartbeat. Which is what life is all about in the end; the unexpected things no one can ever plan for.

One of these six men, that's all you need to know, contacted me with the sad news that his wife had become very, very ill. He went on to elaborate on how her condition was serious and that they were dealing with several doctors and somehow adjusting their lives to handle this crisis and survive it. My heart went out to him and I told him not to worry about the project one iota. Family always comes first here and we stand by that policy with all our creators. If we had to wait for him to complete his contribution, then so be it, we would wait.

I hope you can understand, there was a special team chemistry that has arisen in this project that I immediately realized simply could not be altered. Like a Chef who realizes he has run out of a specific ingredient for his favorite recipe and simply cannot replace it with anything else; no matter how long his hungry customers have to wait, they must. As the months went by, I kept in touch with this creator. On several occasions he strongly suggested I find someone else as to not hold up the rest of the team. I politely, but adamantly, refused to do so, continuing to offer my prayers and support for what he and his wife had to endure.

It was a long ordeal, almost a full year before they could see the light at the end of their horrific tunnel. Doctors at long last were able to put together the proper treatment and drugs and they began to have real hope again. I kept those prayers going out to them.

And now I am so happy to finish this tale with a true, miraculous, happy ending. This fellow's lovely wife is fine, healthy and doing super. He then wasted no time fulfilling his obligation to us and produced a marvelous work that is simply great. This package would incomplete without his talented contribution.

Of course the other heroes in this story are the other five creators who never once, not ever, complained about this book's delay. Each of them are true professionals; kind, considerate gentlemen each possessing genuine nobility. It is my honor to call each a friend and to have been their editor on this book. Thanks to all of you who waited so patiently so that we could produce this awesome book.

Ron Fortier
4/29/2013
Fort Collins, CO
(www.airship27.com)
(Airship27@comcast.net)

Airship 27

GANGSTERS & GUNMOLLS

JIM ANTHONY
SUPER-DETECTIVE

Printed in Great Britain
by Amazon

57884988R00086